I0748322

JEREMIAH'S WIVES

A collection of short stories by
Ray Mawerera

First published in Great Britain in 2025 by:

Carnelian Heart Publishing Ltd
Suite A
82 James Carter Road
Mildenhall
Suffolk
IP28 7DE
UK

www.carnelianheartpublishing.co.uk

Copyright ©Ray Mawerera 2025

Paperback ISBN   978-1-914287-94-7
eBOOK ISBN   978-1-914287-95-4

A CIP catalogue record for this book is available from the British Library.

This collection of short stories is entirely a work of fiction. The names, characters and incidents portrayed in it are the work of the author's imagination. Any resemblance to actual persons, living or dead, is purely coincidental.

All rights reserved. No part of this publication may be reproduced, stored in a retrieval system or transmitted in any form or by any means, electronic, mechanical, photocopying, recording or otherwise without prior written permission from the publisher.

Editors:
Panashe Lazarus Nyagwambo &
Samantha Rumbidzai Vazhure

Cover design:
Artwork - Ganime Dönmez
Layout - Rebeca Covers

Typeset by Carnelian Heart Publishing Ltd
Layout and formatting by DanTs Media

To the memories of my uncle, Malume Joe, and Mukoma Chenjerai Hove, who shared the extraordinary quality of telling funny fables with a serious face. And to Carol, Tina, Chichi and Beezy as well as the crazy siblings TeeJay and Emma, our first grandchildren.

"Things are not always what they seem; the first appearance deceives many; the intelligence of few perceives what has been hidden in the recesses of the mind."

- Phaedrus

Table of Contents

JEREMIAH'S WIVES

"**WHY** is it that when a man amasses wealth, his next actions include marrying more wives?"

Chinebundo knew this was a provocative question when he asked it, but he relished a good debate. Although it was not a new question, it created the buzz that he wanted and was good for passing the time.

It is, indeed, a paradox, the wizened man whose locks had turned an almost white shade of grey observed, doodling in the sand with a twig.

Ah, but it is not strange at all, countered the other men. They sat lazily on makeshift wooden stools under the shady gum tree across the sandy island of hot, dry earth from Musami's Bottle Store & Eatery. It is quite natural and *expected* in fact, they concurred. Our fathers and our fathers' fathers and their fathers before them had many, many wives. There are more women than men. And it is a good thing to have a big family; the only problem is you will need a lot of food, but if you have the means, it is no problem at all. Wealth must be shared, or else the ancestors will take it away. What better way to share it than for one to become an in-law of several families? That way, you see, the son-in-law extends his charity while at the same time, he ensures there are enough heirs to continue his legacy. In any case, it is better to marry your own than to steal other men's fruits or spoil other people's daughters before their time and, worse, refuse to take care of the result. Men must be men and not let their sons wander around like children without totems! There have been far too many totem-less children lately and it is not a good thing.

Chinebundo, whose name had been changed to Hosea by the Catholic missionaries when he converted to Christianity, was the lone voice objecting and quoting bible verses. While the other men passed around a clay pot of maize brew fermented over seven days to reach alcoholic potency, Chinebundo was content with a bottle of Coca-Cola that he was nursing so it would not finish too quickly. No one in the community acknowledged his new name. After all, and in any case, adult men with families were called by their surnames or the names of their first children. His first name mattered little anymore.

Chinebundo was not intimidated by the fact that his was the only voice of reason. The debate gave him the perfect opportunity to teach his fellow men about "The Way". He had ready answers for those that thought they were clever and pointed out David's adulterous sin, Abraham sleeping with his wife's maid, Jacob taking in two wives, and the non-believer's favourite example, King Solomon's 700 wives and 300 concubines.

A private thought made him smile. Here he was,

taking part in a debate on polygamy that he had induced, triggered by village gossip over the businessman Jeremiah. Chinebundo was smiling because the Jeremiah of the bible faced lots of opposition and persecution for saying things the leaders of the community did not want to hear. Yet the bible's Jeremiah was undeterred and was, himself, instructed by God to not marry because it would interfere with his mission. Chinebundo saw himself as that Jeremiah – quite the opposite of the village's Jeremiah of several wives, quite the opposite too, of his own biblical alter ego Hosea, who married a prostitute. Regardless of the irony, this gave Chinebundo even more determination to speak out in the face of fierce counter-arguments. The more they argued, the stronger his resolve to make them repent grew.

The truth of the matter was people either loathed or envied the businessman, Jeremiah, in almost equal measure. Not only had he amassed a vast amount of wealth; he had also lured into his home three of the most sought-after women in the village. The last of them was a smashingly beautiful, small dynamite, little more than half his age, very controversial and fiery in both speech and action. His mother's brother was the only one who could tell how Jeremiah did it, as each time he married, the villagers were seemingly caught unawares. They only found out when they were called to the feast to celebrate the union of Jeremiah to each new wife, and wondered when and how. Jeremiah's uncle, his most trusted confidante, refused to tell. Even members of the delegations that he put together for the *lobola* negotiations were only told on the eve of the assignment, to minimise the chances of the wind prematurely carrying and spreading the news across the village like the seeds of *mutsine*, the blackjack plant.

Sometimes there were whispers and murmurings. It was a public secret that many mothers and fathers wished their daughters could be lured into Jeremiah's lair too. But he seemed very selective, even so cold sometimes that you couldn't "start" him. They said of him that he had a "heavy" character, not easy to make conversation with. Once in his home, his wives, too, became distant and unapproachable, and it was difficult to know for sure what kind of life was lived there. Of course, such inconveniences have never stopped any village's rumour mill and many stories were created about how happy or unhappy Jeremiah's wives were, all dependent, of course, on the inclination of the storyteller.

The businessman himself was never seen at the gatherings of idle minds such as the one at Musami's Bottle Store & Eatery. He was preoccupied with his business, either taking his produce from his farm to the markets in the city, where he would also collect rent from tenants at the two houses he had built there, or going from his butchery to the store and back again, to make sure everything was being run properly. If not, he would be in the Chief's compound, discussing the politics of the village or yet another community project.

Access to Jeremiah's Mansion was through an almost hidden road which he had constructed through the forest and up the iconic Chiutsi Hill, up which it snaked for several hundred metres. Chiutsi Hill – the smoking hill, was named so on account of the heavy smoke-like mist that engulfed the hillock every morning, an enveloping white cloud that dissipated slowly and gradually from dawn, till just after sunup, when it made way for daylight to reveal the natural wonder on which Jeremiah's Mansion sat ensconced. Once up there, the visitor would be confronted by a high stone wall and a large, black double gate of solid steel on wheels. Up ahead, the imposing structure that was the mansion looked palatial, especially considering Jeremiah had added semi-detached wings to it to match the growth of his family. One of these dwellings stood distinctly apart from the others, drawing instant attention to itself through the sparsely spread trees in the courtyard. A huge succulent of the aloe family, famed for its multipurpose wellness qualities, stood as an iconic landmark that interrupted the courtyard view, where the family's vehicle fleet appeared randomly parked.

From just inside the steel gates would emerge a security man in a sailor's cap and matching khakis, slowly and affectedly brandishing a baton stick across an open palm, to inquire on your business before allowing you to enter. It was just for show, for the guard's own personal gratification: it seemed important to him to demonstrate some authority, although it was not necessary. People were hardly denied entry, except suspicious characters for which the guard, a former policeman, had a keen eye and thus, on that score, had his uses. Most of the time, Jeremiah allowed people to enter, knowing that coming up the slopes of that hill was not for the faint-hearted and anyone braving the climb had a genuine reason to do so. He was famed for his generosity but also knew when he was being taken for a ride. People said it was this discerning mind that had made him the successful businessman that he was.

Jeremiah's Mansion was a sight to behold. One could, in fact, espy it from the village below, especially spectacular at night, when all the lights were switched on. Being the keenly astute businessman that he was, the only other place such lights were seen was at the Chief's compound, where Jeremiah had donated a solar-powered electricity system almost similar to his and ensured his engineers kept it well-maintained. That made Jeremiah almost formidable as a perceived de facto Chief's Adviser and, therefore, power broker. That is what was said in the village. If Jeremiah himself looked at it that way, he did a good job of not exploiting it openly...

JEREMIAH

I did not set out to marry many wives. I was quite happy with Selina, the girl I went to high school with, right there in the village where we were both born and raised. People talk. I have heard the whispers. There is nothing you can do about that.

Selina and I did not talk much in school at first, apart from greetings when we met in class. I knew I liked her from the time I saw her when I joined the class in my first year in secondary school. She seemed so... well-mannered and gently beautiful, if you can imagine such. She was quiet and reserved but I wouldn't quite say she was shy. In class, she spoke very little and only to answer the period teacher's questions, almost always correctly, regardless of the subject. Selina was smart.

She sat in the third row in the column along the windows, where she spent most of the time looking outside, towards the playground. When everyone was playful during breaks, Selina would sit quietly in her space, chewing her pencil or pen and looking outside. She was always looking outside, even if there was nothing there except little birds flying up and down and running along, pecking for worms or whatever it is birds look for in the ground.

The first time I gathered enough courage to speak to her during one of those breaks, she did not seem at all surprised. The desk in front of her was empty. I think the boy who sat there was absent because of some illness, but I cannot remember fully. I sat on the desk facing her, using the boy's chair as a footstool, and greeted her. She smiled up at me warmly and said, "How are you, Jerry?"

It is difficult to describe what happened to my heart then, the way she cooed and said my name like no one else had, before or since. You must remember that we were young and changes were taking place in our bodies that were as exciting as they were scary. I asked her why she was always looking out the window even when there was nothing to see. She shrugged and said, "You might not see it. As for me, it is better to fill up that empty space with my imagination than to be part of the circus in here. And those birds always look so happy, always showing so much freedom."

Ah, freedom! Did Selina yearn for such freedom? Her words sounded very clever and I did not answer immediately. Later, I would make fun of the fact that she said "as for me" quite a lot! Instead, I studied her features and decided that I had been right about her natural beauty. I smiled at my own thoughts.

She smiled back. "You're staring too much, Jerry. And why are you smiling like that?"

Unfortunately, the next teacher came in and I had to go back to my desk. But from then on, Selina and I would steal glances and smiles at each other from across the room and exchange wordless messages. The day after that first conversation, we went out onto the school playground shades over lunch break to share the contents of our lunch boxes. Our friendship grew slowly but surely. It felt natural and God-given, and I knew instinctively she was the one.

But then Selina's family moved and she had to be transferred to a new school. We wrote to each other for some time and then, as time passed, the letters became fewer and far between. After secondary school, I moved to the big city's university and took up business studies. University life is intense and can sweep you along in that wave of forceful intensity and high drama. Sometimes you might not even realise what you are doing while you are doing it. You are just doing what everyone else is doing, to fit in and not be labelled. A lot happened and I will confess, yes, there were a lot of distractions, and that's all I'm willing to say. The letters stopped altogether after Selina wrote five that I did not find time to respond to. She almost became a mere memory of an innocent high school flirtation.

Yet it wasn't. In my third year at the university, I went on an errand to the shops while on holiday in our village, and who do I bump into in Mangwende Store but a much more beautiful and buxom version of my school years Selina!

She recognised me first.

"Jerry?" she said, inclining her head when she joined the short line in which I was standing, waiting to pay for groceries. I had turned around impassively to see who had come in behind me.

By the way, in all my life since I was born, only one person ever shortened my name, and that person was Selina. Everyone else – my parents, siblings, neighbours, schoolmates, everyone – called me, fully, Jeremiah. My heart did the same thing it had done when she first asked me how I was all those many years ago.

"Selina!" I exclaimed and we hugged and laughed and swung each other, attracting everyone's attention.

Selina pushed me away gently, suddenly realising the environment we were in and remembering that such public displays of affection only had their place in the city, where she said her family had relocated to when her father got a job in a plastics manufacturing factory. She herself was training as a nurse at the teaching hospital and was about to finish her studies.

That is how Selina and I reconnected. There were lots of stories to share and apologies to exchange over our mutual lack of communication. We forgave and assured each other that we had not forgotten and, although we had had some casual flirtations, that is all they were, and there had been nothing serious.

"As for me, there is not much to tell. My life is not as full of adventure as yours."

She still had the same old sarcasm! I laughed at how some things never changed. Selina laughed with me but seemed reluctant to share whether she was seeing anyone during our time apart. I did not press, seeing as I had not been a saint myself.

Semester breaks can be long and boring if you are in the village and have few or no friends. Selina got pregnant and only discovered it some month or so after going back to her nursing school. For some reason, she chose to break the news at the next semester break, when it was visible for all to see that she was with child. I was unprepared and went to ask mother's brother, who is very close to me, what I should do. He regarded me for a while and then asked me if I loved her. He did not wait for my answer and remarked that she was a decent girl who came from a respected family.

My uncle set the traditional processes in motion and took some family members from my father's side to Selina's family where, after initial confrontation, they paid the appropriate penalties and I got officially married to Selina. I was still in school and was not quite ready, but I had made my own bed and now had to lie in it. My father said so, his sister said so, my mother said so, her brother said so, my grandmother said so, everybody said so. That's all there was to it and there was no argument. What I discovered, which I hadn't known up to then, was that Selina was the girl every mother in the village wanted their son to marry and they were dismayed that she was pregnant by me, even though people had seen us together. Why did they think I didn't deserve her? Surely, they all knew Selina and I loved each other in an inseparable way that everyone even gossiped about? This discovery made me loathe the people of my village for a while. From then on, I resolved to keep them as far away from my private life as community principles allowed.

In the next year, after Selina had been moved to our family homestead, her aunties and mine arranged that she be taken back to her family so she could give birth amongst her own kin, as is tradition. While there, Selina fell sick at the crucial moment and almost died while giving birth. The child did not make it, and she was very sad and depressed for a long time.

I did what I could to comfort her and assured her that it was not her fault, that she wasn't weak and that, sometimes, God does things we do not understand. She cried endlessly, blaming herself for falling pregnant before the proper things were done and that now, her ancestors were punishing her for behaving like a prostitute. These were hard words that ate me up too. I vowed that I would make it up to her and look after her as best as I could.

Selina became worse, to the point where she refused to let me touch her anymore. I was now working and saving up so I could have enough to look after the large family that I dreamt of us having. In time, I managed to open a small convenience tuck shop of my own at the village centre, which did very well because I was selling things people wanted. One day Mr Mangwende, the owner of the grocery store nearby, came to tell me that he was old and retiring and he wanted me to take over his store because he had seen that I was serious about business. Just like that! A month and a half later, I had the store and opened another one six months after that, but I ended up turning it into a butchery instead. I kept the store I got from Mr Mangwende because, if you remember, that is where Selina and I reconnected, so it had sentimental value to me. My fortunes rose and business was good. It was only at home that things were not going well.

I went to visit the chief and the headman and pleaded

with them to let me build on Chiutsi Hill, so that my
dear wife might benefit from the change in the
environment, away from the village gossip. With my
older brother, James, we took with us ample groceries
and two live goats, and the village leaders were happy
and persuaded. Chiutsi was not a sacred hill and there
were no spirits of ancestors roaming around on it. They
had no reason to turn down my request. The presents
also helped them to decide.

Chiutsi Hill was everything I could wish for and
more. The air up here was clean and cool and I had so
much space. I decided to build a mansion to which I
could add other structures, if necessary, without dulling
the design. I got some really creative landscapers from
the city to do the grounds, only clearing away the trees
where the buildings would go. On any day, we were
surrounded by perfect peace, with a cool wind blowing
and the natural sounds of birds and insects giving us a
free orchestra of therapeutic forest sounds. I was most
pleased with the result and Selina congratulated me, but
she remained deadpan and inexpressive.

She seemed fine and even happy when I organised a
huge wedding celebration for us since I could now afford
it. I wanted it to be memorable and I wanted her to be in
no doubt that I loved her. Up to this day, people still talk
about that wedding. Within two days after the guests
left, however, Selina returned to her morose self, and I
felt defeated.

By the fifth year after the stillbirth, I had acquired a
farm 10 kilometres away, and could be said to be
relatively wealthy. These material things meant little to
me though. I was trying to make Selina happy, and it

was not working. I was, at this point, also getting restless and agitated. I wanted a family and it seemed Selina had decided she was not going to try again. The pressure from parents, aunts and some of my siblings also didn't help. Some of it was even insensitive, particularly from my younger sister, Ruth.

One day while at one of our many casual family gatherings, the babies of my brothers and sisters were running around playfully, with the usual happy attention from the adults that only children can attract. Ruth made a cheeky, snide remark and said, "When Mukoma Jeremiah and *makoti* decide to have theirs, *pachanakidza pano!*"

Everyone threw daggers at Ruth who pretended that she had said the most natural thing about the added fun of Selina and I having our own babies. Selina withdrew into herself. Aunty Marina went to her after a reasonable time and took her away to the kitchen under one excuse or other, but everyone saw through it. Uncle looked at me sternly to stop me from reacting. I got up and walked to the chicken coop to tell the chickens how I wished things were different. Some of them stopped and stared at me suspiciously, beaks open as if in surprise, eyes blinking, heads at an enquiring angle… and then resumed their pecking and running around and scratching the ground like *gure* dancers. Our people have a saying: a man does not decline food because of another man's problems.

I cannot say Ruth did not like Selina; I just think she felt Selina relegated her to an ordinary "one of Jeremiah's sisters". You see, growing up, Ruth and I were very close and I doted on her quite some. When Selina and I got married, she was the happiest of sisters. She danced like she was high on something and ululated the most. At some point, though, the reality of Selina moving in hit her. That's when she started behaving like this.

The pressure ate me up in a big way. So, one day, at a traditional field celebration to coax the ancestors to bring us a good rainy season, I asked my uncle about a young lady who occasionally came to the butchery to buy meat. My uncle, who could read me like a book, looked at me slyly and asked me to describe her. I had studied her well and, if asked, could draw her face from memory, so it was not a challenge for me to do so. Uncle laughed out loud, as if I had said the most nonsensically hilarious thing.

"Natsai, virgin daughter of Musami," he pronounced, shook his head and laughed again before he declared, matter-of-factly, "You can't get that one, my sister's son. Especially not you, a married man with no child. Do you know what people are saying?" My uncle is one of those people who can say anything to me and not care how I feel about it.

After he said what he said, I am afraid to say, I resolved to entrap Natsai. I made sure I was in the butchery when she next came for her meat purchase and surprised her by greeting her by her first name. I gave her three extra kilograms and told her to tell her mother it was a present from me, as a thank-you for their loyal custom. She did not say anything and kept staring at me with a smile of… confusion? Disbelief? I kept a straight face and noticed she looked back several times as she hurried home. The seed had been sown.

I met Mr Musami one day not quite two weeks later

while walking to the chief's compound. Like Mr Mangwende, his peer, Mr Musami had retired from the retail business and surrendered his bottle store and eatery to a nephew. It was one of those businesses you grow up seeing as a local landmark feature that hardly changes, either in outlook or format, regardless of other changes around it – the same yesterday, today and tomorrow!

Mr Musami stopped me and got off his bicycle, shook my hand and thanked me for the meat. A slight man with high cheekbones and deep, piercing eyes, he held my hand for a while, peering at me closely, then said, "You're a good man, son of Mangosho. People don't know. They just talk about places they did not visit or spend the day. But the ancestors see and know, and God will bless you. Do not change, remain as you are. You are a good man. Do not change." He let me go and I continued on my way. I was elated and congratulated myself on my decision to walk instead of drive to the chief's compound. From then onwards, except for the day I drove the new pickup truck that I had bought for him, I never drove to see the chief. I considered this encounter an omen.

Some months passed. I surprised Natsai once more one day when she came to the store by announcing to her that I was going to send my people to her people. She giggled and said she thought I was crazy. Tellingly and encouragingly for me, she did not object and gave me a shy, sidewise glance and smile. I never revealed my true feelings for her, except little hints that I delivered as playful jibes. I always tried to find ways for her to linger, but I also think she liked these encounters as she made little effort to get away. Plus, she reacted very well to my jibes, by which I mean… well, she knew what she knew and laughed appropriately each time. I repeated my "threat" about my people visiting hers several times more but received the same giggly responses, until this one day when she came in and I think she had had counsel from an aunt.

"We will see when they come," was her response finally, and my heart jumped. *Here come the children,* my heart sang!

I resolved to do things properly. I had to tell Selina first. Timing was of the essence. My chance came at the beginning of winter, one day when she seemed calmer than what had become her normal. She was sitting cross-legged across the sitting room, warming herself at the fireplace. Like I said, I had built a good house, following the designs I had seen in the city. I knew Selina liked the house and it made me happy that she approved, even though she showed little emotion. She has never been materialistic.

"Selina, my wife," I began and cleared my throat.

She started, then smiled. I stiffened. She had not smiled in a long time. I hesitated. She released me from my mental prison.

"Jerry, my husband," she said softly. "I know you love me, so don't be afraid to say anything. You and I, we have come a long way. What is it?"

I hesitated again. I nodded and swallowed and stammered, "It… it… it is very good, very g-good my wife to know that you know th-that I love you…"

Selina rested her head on her left shoulder and squinted at me. Once she had seen what she had seen from that angle, she got up slowly and came to the sofa where I was sitting. She knelt in front of me and took my hands. She did not speak. She just looked up at me, the beginnings of tears in her soft eyes. She did not blink, and I found it hard to look away though I felt afraid. Two streams of tears oozed slowly down her cheeks. Selina ignored them.

Finally, she nodded, leaned forward and cupped my face in her hands. "I understand. It's ok."

I was taken aback. What was she saying was ok?

"You want to marry someone else, isn't it Jerry? Who is it?"

This is the way women are gifted, to know things that are hidden. But I had no time to think about that then. I took the plunge and blurted it out. It was now or never. I poured out streams of apologies as I asked for her permission and told her it wasn't because I loved her less but that I wanted children and she wasn't, er… I wouldn't- I couldn't finish and kept repeating my apologies. I have never felt so awkward in my life.

Selina was as calm as the river on a quiet summer day. She got up, returned to her fireplace, where she resumed her sitting position, and stared into the fire with a very composed expression on her face. The tears dried of their own accord. She looked relieved. Strange woman indeed.

The ceremony to marry Natsai went smoothly and she was brought to my homestead as Second Wife. Out of respect for Selina, I made sure that the wedding ceremony, while lavish and generously put together, would not outshine the one I had for her. Selina received her calmly, a sign of matronly maturity. Natsai was unsure and remained uneasy in the first few weeks, trying to figure out what Selina thought deep down. But as the time rolled by, the homestead became peaceful and everyone seemed happy. Selina played big sister to Natsai and taught her a few chores that the younger woman was not so good at. Sometimes I would arrive from my stores or the farm to find my two wives busying themselves in the kitchen or outside, exchanging conversation or laughing at some joke.

Then, good news. My wives got pregnant around the same time, towards the end of the year. The two sons came a month apart, in April and May. It was a happy homestead and it made me happy.

Then I made an inexcusable blunder. This was purely my fault and I take full responsibility. Even my uncle was very harsh in his condemnation of my thoughtlessness. He told me in no uncertain terms that a man who used the stick between his legs to think was a fool of the highest order and deserved all the punishment that the heavens and the ancestors meted on him. He told me I was a disgrace and that he was ashamed to have me as the son of his sister, a respected member of the women's fellowship at church and mentor to many young women and girls. How did I think she would be able to face the pastor's wife, not to mention all those other women? Had money made me a fool to that extent? The way he put it, I became very ashamed and humbled. I told uncle I was sorry, I did not know what had come over me but what could I do? It was spilt milk that could not be collected again. My father would not speak to me and mother sided with him. It was pathetic and miserable.

But it was alright in the end, I'm sure because of the possibility of the number of grandchildren to celebrate and show off growing. It is a reality in my country that men's statures grow correspondingly with their wealth as measured by the number of children, grandchildren and animals one has.

Evelyn is the only one of my wives who did not grow up in the village. She's a town girl, who only came to the village occasionally to visit her grandparents. She was a petite, light-skinned girl, very beautiful to look at, with long, flowing hair and bushy eyebrows. She had small hairs on her arms and legs and even the traces of a thin moustache that made her very attractive indeed. She was also slightly bow-legged but carried her rather short frame very well, usually in high shoes – not the heels that would make it impossible to walk in the village sand and stone pathways, but with enough height to make up for that shortcoming.

Even as I marvelled at the magnificence of her sultry daintiness, I told myself that the age gap that separated us rendered any connection mere fantasy.

She was young and exuberant, too much so to be ignored. She would shout greetings and wave at people as she passed them, her carefree attitude resulting in wide smiles as they waved back – followed by conspiratorial huddles of gossip after she had passed. On the occasions that I saw her, I wished I was younger, but I knew it was just lustful thinking. Of course, I allowed myself the occasional indulgence of the delusion. What man doesn't dream, even of the unattainable? But she was too young, and I laughed at myself often for entertaining the hallucination, for that is what it was.

The men and women in the village talk a lot and I picked up that, although she could easily win a beauty contest in the village and came from a decent family, she would be a handful for any man. Such was the free spirit in her which she acquired from traveling across the seas. It made me curious.

And the world has its own tricks. I finally and unexpectedly found myself dancing with her at a fundraising dinner that the aspiring local member of parliament staged at the village hall, where all the businessmen and prominent people in the village had been invited. The aspiring MP, who did have village support of significance as a homeboy, said the money raised was to put electricity at the local school so he could bring computers there and allow the school to catch up with modern times.

She came at me, the boldness of it! In the amusement of the moment, I did not ask if she had come with anyone or had her own invitation. At the time, I was in fact contemplating returning home after registering my presence and making my donation. I had gone there alone because my wives were heavily pregnant at the time. This was not my kind of event. I do not like huge crowds. Besides, I seemed to be getting drunk.

She was a very good dancer and taught me a few movements. I inhaled the alluring fragrance of her sweet perfume as she told me, during the dances, that she knew me very well but I did not know her because I was too proud. She told me she thought I considered myself above everyone else in the village, which is why I hardly spoke to anyone. Everyone in the village knew of my arrogance, she accused, but in ever-seductive tones. I had to lean down to catch her soft whispers above the music. I'm told now that we painted a picture of intimacy to other guests as we swayed slowly to the music – her in my arms looking sweetly up at me and me leaning down into her face to catch what she was saying. Looking back, I cannot help thinking she probably wanted them to think that way too. Still, I am left wondering what business it was of theirs and whether they were there for the party or to watch what everyone else was doing.

She shared my drink or, rather, helped herself to it – I was one of the few people drinking whisky – and, at some stage, dragged me outside. For some air, she said, as it was getting too hot inside. She led me to my car parked at the far end of the grounds, perhaps to illustrate that she, indeed, knew me. So, we got to know each other. Although I felt a little guilt, I blamed the alcohol and dismissed it as one of those things that happen to a man challenged by a flirtatious woman. We experienced such girls during my university years. I pushed it out of my mind but did notice people's looks right from the very next day. The village gossip machine was in full swing, and I ignored it, as usual. For her part, Evelyn disappeared, and I reasoned she had gone back to the comfortable non-intrusiveness of city suburbia. It suited me well for I was not sure what I would say to her after that incident.

My celebration turned out to be an illusion. She arrived at my homestead up on Chiutsi some months later, pushing a small belly in front of her, only a few months after the birth of the second of my sons. Fortuitously, Selina's had come first and without any trouble this time. The air of celebration was still pervasive at my residence, and it had become a place of peace and happiness.

Evelyn's arrival was a spoiler. To say it was not

pleasant at all is a major understatement, but I couldn't deny the pregnancy, knowing what I knew about that night of spontaneous, lustful gratification, during which the question of protection was neither spoken of nor considered. The arithmetic made sense. Selina and Natsai were not impressed and, I must say, gave her hell from the day she arrived. It was my responsibility. Not for the first time, I had made my bed, even if it had thorns in it. Selina in particular shocked me. I had never seen her so angry and it really got to me. She even called me Jeremiah! I had never heard her utter my first name in full. This was the first time ever that I had angered the love of my life and I felt terrible. I had really blown it. Natsai supported her and was even more frenzied. It was war in the compound, and it was too much for me. I was hit by a fear and panic that I had never experienced. And so, I pretended to be a man in control.

As soon as I found the chance to speak, I wore my sternest face and told Selina and Natsai very roughly to take it or leave it, that they had to accept that there were now three of them. Whoever found it unacceptable knew what to do. On and on I thundered and blew. But deep down, I was afraid that, being women of principle, they might just take me up on my challenge, call my bluff. What would I do then? I was nothing without them. My life would become meaningless. When I stormed off, I drove very fast from Chiutsi, creating my own cloud of dust when I hit the gravel outside the gate. It's a wonder I did not crash. I drove straight to the farm and stayed there the entire weekend, but no serious thinking ever came to me. It was just a journey of self-pity, shame and embarrassment. I had declared to my wives that I would marry Evelyn, and I would do it, although she had not been in my plans. Besides, I could not fathom the idea of having a child out there roaming around as if it didn't have a father. We had enough of them in the village as it was. It was a topic the chief and I had discussed times without number, and I am no hypocrite, nor did I want to disappoint or embarrass him by not walking my talk.

It meant that Uncle had another job to do, one that he really didn't relish this time. I told him I was going to marry Evelyn and braved the lecture. After making sure I knew exactly what he thought of the whole sordid affair, Uncle executed the job quickly, as if handling hot coals. It just seemed weird that Evelyn's people welcomed us with no condemnation or any of the traditional punishments that we had prepared for. It was as if they expected this, indeed embraced it… as a god-send, perhaps?

EVELYN

I honestly do not know what the fuss is about. People are just too old-fashioned. I am a go-getter and I know what I want. My parents raised me to be self-focused and independent minded. When I see something that I want, I just go out and grab it. Rural people are not used to seeing such independence, especially from young women like me. They are too primitive.

When I visited my grandparents in the summer before last and heard about Jeremiah, I had just come from Oakland, California, in the United States of America. Those people in the village do not even know where America is, to start with. I doubt if any of them have ever seen an aeroplane, apart from the occasional ones that fly over the village. Of course, I am not including my Jeremiah, the only enlightened person there. If it wasn't for him, those two other stupid wives of his would not have come close to an airport. Sometimes I wonder how, with his university education and such a brilliant mind, he ended up with such SRBs, but I guess there wasn't much to choose from in that backwater they call a village.

There is too much primitive gossip from the idle minds of the village. Let me put the record straight: I am not a desperate gold-digger. I am a fully qualified and degreed cosmetologist from a reputable American university. In America, I learned that if you don't stand up for yourself, no one else will. No one, alright? Right now, I am finished with the interior decorations for my first cosmetology business within a high-end mall just on the outskirts of the capital city, towards the village. It's a deliberate location, sited to capture the shamelessly rich wives and girlfriends of the well-heeled, who choose to build multimillion-dollar mansions as far away from everyone else as possible. It suits me fine. I will be able to charge what I want for stroking their egos. Fortunately, it's not too long a drive from our palace but long enough for me to enjoy the breeze in my Brazilian hair when I open the sunroof of the red Mercedes Benz Coupe that my Jeremiah bought me, complete with white leather interiors.

Everything I have done and got was well planned, deliberate and systematic. I have no regrets. Fortune favours the brave. I knew, when I first heard about Jeremiah from my grandparents, that fate had brought me here and he was just what I needed to kickstart my business, which I had been encouraged to pursue in college.

I do not like village life, ordinarily. I only go there because I love my grandparents and enjoy the way they pamper me. Other than that, the pace is too slow for me. The people are too inquisitive and, anyone who is not familiar with them will mistake that as good hospitality. It is not. They like poking their noses into other people's affairs. I deal with them by just waving and grinning when I see them staring. Those people can stare, *yoh*! I am glad my father took us away from there to live in the city when we were little. In the city, our house was surrounded by a high wall, and we did not have nosy neighbours coming to borrow salt. It was peaceful.

Our palace on Misty Hill is almost as peaceful. Almost. There are those two retrogrades to spoil it all. I complained to Jeremiah and he built my wing well away from their semi-detached nonsense. They are birds of a feather, with primitive qualifications. Anyone can be a nurse these days and teachers are a laughingstock, what with their measly pay. Of course, I would not say this to their faces, nor to Jeremiah. I am not stupid. Although the first wife, Selina, tries to be nice to me, she's a freaky religious bore and too perfect. Look, I sympathise that she lost her first child, ok? But life deals one hard blow sometimes. It's just reality and you have to take the bitter with the sweet. The other one, the teacher, Natsai, that one and I will never get along. She's a shameless gossip and has made some stupid accusations that I am a slut. I hear these things. I should sue her but I really do not have time for such blabbermouths. She keeps boasting about how pure she was when Jeremiah married her.

There is nothing fantastic about being married a virgin. It doesn't make you a saint and, if anything, shows just how slow you are. These are not the sixties.

As casually as I could, so as not to draw suspicion, I got my grandparents to tell me about this rich dude, Jeremiah, and made a few special visits past his businesses, once or twice actually walking in and buying something. I did not speak to him but I liked what I saw. He was a very private man. I like private men. I found out also that he was quite powerful, being a friend of the Chief and all. I love power. Above all, he was rich. I needed start-up for my business and, given what I had already heard about his generosity, Jeremiah would be the perfect sponsor.

This business that people say he's twice my age what-what, that's all primitive. Love does not know age. Jeremiah is as cute as his money and his age means nothing. After all…

Anyway, I overheard *sekuru* telling *ambuya* about the big fundraising event at the village hall, where only the rich and famous were invited. I was at the sink just by the open kitchen outside, doing the dishes under the moonlight. What? You think I don't do such domestic things? Prejudices!

"Funny," I announced as casually as you like, going in and wiping the water off my hands on my village skirt. I look like a proper village girl when I want to. "Mr Jeremiah invited me to that party."

It was my way of trying to confirm if they knew or had heard if he was going. My grandparents looked at each other. Grandma said, "Mr Jeremiah? You speak to that man?"

"Why not?" I shot back. "I went and introduced myself to him when you told me about him. You made him sound interesting."

"He doesn't speak to strangers," Grandpa said.

"I am not a stranger. Not any more at least."

"He is too old for you. What do you want from him?"

"And he is a very married man, Eve, very married. Two wives."

Grandma doesn't pronounce the short form of my name the way that you are pronouncing it. She is too rural for that. She says it the way it is spelt, E-VEH.

"Why is that important?" I said offhandedly. "Anyway, I accepted his invitation and I am going."

If it matters, the truth is that I had not even had direct contact with Jeremiah and there had been no such invitation. I was just going to try my luck and get close to him. I'm a go-getter, I told you. So, on the day, I dolled myself up as sexily attractive as I could without looking too indecent, walked to the village hall which was not too far away and saw Jeremiah's huge SUV parked conveniently at the most secluded parking spot outside the hall. You couldn't mistake it: it was the only one of its kind in the village. The party had already started, and I congratulated myself for brilliant timing; one must always be fashionably late to make the right impact. After some time, I approached the entrance and, employing my most disarming smile, told the muscles manning it that I was Mr Jeremiah's guest. They didn't argue. I am confident like that. And too pretty to gate-crash parties.

A band was playing and people were on the dance

floor. Except Jeremiah, who stood alone to one side, sipping a glass of what I found out later to be single malt whisky. Perfect. I ignored the stares and waltzed my way to him slowly and introduced myself, "Hi, I'm Evelyn."

He regarded me with what I thought was amusement, looked me up and down and nodded.

"Hmm. Do I know you?" he asked. I shook my head slowly and just smiled back as sweetly as I could. I extended my hand and took the glass out of his. He didn't resist. He watched me gently and slowly rub the rim of the glass with my index finger, take a sip, then gaze at him over the top of the glass with a naughty smile on my face. I copied all this from some American movie, I can't remember which. I think it worked.

He beckoned to a waiter, ordered another glass and indicated for him to fill up the one I had. In a few minutes I had him laughing at my little seductive insults, captive, eating straight out of my hands. I am not a slut but, like I told you, I am a confident woman and I know what I want. I was determined to get my start-up capital.

It was never my intention to do it the way it happened in the end. It's just that, well, the whisky… We danced and I suddenly started feeling horny. I flirted with him, we got drunk and I think I persuaded him to go outside to his car. I remember telling him it was getting too hot inside the hall. He didn't protest. We made love in the car and he drove me home. These things happen. When I think back on this incident, I smile.

My true intentions were to use the fundraiser purely to introduce myself to Jeremiah. A few weeks, maybe a month or two after that incident, just as I was planning to go to the village again for the weekend to reacquaint myself with Jeremiah and present my business proposal, I started feeling funny and nauseous. I took a self-test and my fears were confirmed. I visited my gynaecologist and she confirmed too that, yes, I was a few weeks pregnant. What are the chances of that? Unbelievable.

I was raised Catholic and there was never any question of getting rid of it. Besides, I am not one to wallow in regret. Instead of beating myself up for being careless, I accepted my fate and told my aunt, and she told everyone else. I got a thorough tongue lashing and was called all sorts of names, but I noticed they toned down when I told them whose it was. Also, I reminded them what my grandmother had told me about accepting one's fate: coughing does not remove a pregnancy. What was important was how to move forward.

In case you think like those witches, there is no question that it belonged to Jeremiah. I have to tell you that when I returned from the States, I was completely unattached. None of the boys I saw or met were my type and most of them were broke anyway. Sure, I wasn't pure and all, and I might know how to flirt, but I respect and value myself: people like me don't come on the cheap and are not for just anyone. My grandma did a great job teaching me life stuff.

After the initial shock, I congratulated myself. Even if Jeremiah were to refuse to marry me, he would have to look after his child. Opportunity! Life gives you lemons, you make lemonade, that's what I learned in America.

When my bump became visible my folks said they were kicking me out of the house. It didn't look good and people were beginning to talk, they said. I did not protest when my aunt came and we took the first bus to the village, timing our journey so that we walked up the hill as the sun sank into the horizon.

There was a guard at the gate. He was a suspicious fellow. Of course, today he grovels and worships the very ground I walk on. My aunt is as stubborn as me and had us sit just outside that gate until he went and summoned his boss.

Jeremiah remembered me, thankfully. I would have been surprised, though, if I had not made an impression. Almost a year later, one morning after he slept over at mine, I was the one to be surprised when he revealed that he pretended not to know me at the party. He had seen me before but had decided to leave me well alone, until that night when I bulldozed myself into his world. I was a little mortified at being beaten at my own game but had to marvel at Jeremiah's chess player mind. I wondered what could have happened if I had not got pregnant.

The two wives were hysterically enraged when I arrived. But my aunt left me there and returned home. It was up to Jeremiah to handle his situation. It's been three years now, but those two witches still hate me. There is nothing I can do about that. They laughed at first when they found out that my child was a girl, but I have a boy coming. Now they are quiet. They'll come around. I've been doing my best to reach out to them and even offered them free grooming. They need it. I heard them laughing behind my back the first time I made my offer and they pretended to be civil. But they'll come around. I am as much Jeremiah's wife as they are, whether they like it or not. They must just deal with it.

NATSAI

Daddy Jeremiah wronged us. That's the honest truth. Sometimes Maiguru Selina and I sit and talk about the whole shock of it. We hadn't expected our husband to humiliate us like that. She's an uppity slut with a terrible attitude. Everything about her is wrong. She shouldn't be here. Maiguru Selina and I are worried that she will have a bad effect on our children, so we try to shield them from her. It's just that children are children and, when we are not looking, our boys call her little girl to play on the slide and swings at the bottom end of the yard near the orchard.

I have noticed, however, that she has been trying to be nice lately. The other day, she came to visit us and announced that she was opening a studio to enhance women's beauty. She offered us some beauty treatment. We were in a good mood that day and didn't want to spoil our day, so we told her that it was nice of her and we would be ready once she had everything in place. When she left, we laughed and shook our heads. We have no need for make-up or to enhance anything. Daddy Jeremiah married us for our natural looks, that much we know and it makes us proud.

She's also too materialistic. That woman worships money. That's the difference between her and us. Look at Maiguru Selina. She told me her story. She and our husband were high school sweethearts and I know they married for love when Daddy Jeremiah had nothing. I respect Maiguru Selina and I am grateful to her for allowing me to come into her space when I didn't deserve to.

I am also grateful to Daddy Jeremiah for respecting my family and giving me dignity when he proposed to marry me. He explained fully to me and I understood the challenges he and Maiguru Selina were going through. He seemed miserable and I was moved by his honesty. I wanted to help. And so, I saved myself for him and waited patiently. Tete, my father's sister, told me that a virtuous woman is patient. Although he loves me in his special way, Daddy Jeremiah never pretended that he did not love his first wife. He was just anxious about her and that after so many years of marriage, there was still no child.

Daddy Jeremiah is a strong but soft, generous and charming man, and I was drawn to him. I feel safe and secure under his love and care. He turned me from a girl into a woman, and made my parents happy too, because he did everything properly. He never forced himself on me and I just love the way he set everything in motion, from the jokes in the store right through to the day when everyone sat under the tree at my parents' house. I'll never forget that. It was like a dream come true and I know people envied me, but also that I made my parents proud. My father had said for a long time that Daddy Jeremiah was a gentleman and hard worker, unlike some of the men in the village who only met at his bottle store to drink and gossip like women at the community well. When the proposal came, it was not hard for my father to accept and I was happy that he was happy.

It took only a few months after I joined them for Maiguru Selina and I to really get along and trust each other. I am also grateful to God for placing me here, because Maiguru Selina relaxed and was able to conceive, at last. After that, we became inseparable, Maiguru Selina and I. And I saw, too, that the colour had come back into Daddy Jeremiah's face. It made me happy. Our house was now a proper home.

He worked much harder than he had done in previous years and the farm had a bumper harvest of maize and wheat that year. The animals also did well and none of them got sick. It seemed everything was designed to create happiness in our household. By the time the babies came, Daddy Jeremiah had rewarded us with renovations to our two beautiful houses. Now the house on top of Chiutsi Hill looked more imposing, grander. Maiguru Selina's bit was slightly larger, with an extra bedroom and separate shower, but I was fine with that. Daddy Jeremiah also wanted to buy each of us a car but when he told us, we asked him not to spend too much money unnecessarily, there were the children's futures to think of. Instead, we asked him to buy one car, since we were always together. And that is what happened. We go everywhere together and it's a big enough machine, which we take turns to drive into the village, or to town or to the farm with our children so they also learn farm life and the importance of working hard. Most of the time, however, we just drive each other to work, sometimes one dropping the other off or vice-versa. Daddy Jeremiah never insisted for us to stop working, as rich as he is. He argues that our jobs are important because they benefit the community. This is wise and true. I am happy when the kids I teach pass. And Maiguru Selina keeps everybody healthy and manages their pain. They all love her and think she is a hero.

When Maiguru Selina is working shifts, it's not a problem for us because her shifts start long after I have finished the day's work and finish when I have to start the following day. We are comfortable, Maiguru Selina and I.

Were comfortable.

It all changed when that little slut came, with her insatiable appetite for money and sex, and our cosy life was turned upside down.

She thinks we're envious of her. She's lost and very mistaken. But then, she's too young to even understand how to stay in a marriage. Or that vanity kills. One day she's going to fall so hard that the noise she makes will echo around the village. No one will sympathise. Everyone knows that she thinks village people are stupid. She calls our place Misty Hill when the whole village knows it's Chiutsi. So vain! Everyone knows that she married Daddy Jeremiah for his money and was so shameless she set him up. I am not wishing her ill but she is bad news. Even the car she chose is to show off. All those drives she takes into the city purporting to be running errands for her business… one day, the truth will come out. Several times, I have seen her talking to the chief's eldest son and she's going to create war between our husband and the chief if she continues her stupidity.

Daddy Jeremiah threatened us when we objected to her arrival. We don't normally raise our voices to our husband, but we could see what he could not see. We are women and we saw through her from the beginning. Either he's too blind, or he is pretending. Anyway, he is the man of the house. It's enough that he looks after us well. We are only happy we have each other, Maiguru Selina and I.

SELINA

It's all my fault. If I had not been selfish and stubborn, if I had not tried to draw everyone else into my misery as if they were equally guilty, Jerry would have the happiness that we talked about when we were kids in high school, and we would have lived our dream lives. But I was selfish and stupid.

I was not surprised when he told me he was intending to marry a second wife. I expected it and was only surprised that it had taken him so long. I was also surprised that he did not divorce me. I marvel at Jerry. He has a huge heart. He has patience. I believe Jerry loves me. He made this one huge mistake that we all regret for him, but I have long forgiven him for that.

Natsai is finding it difficult. I think she is still to understand Jerry. He is not one to make excuses for his own mistakes or try to shift the blame elsewhere. He is a real man, who takes responsibility for his actions, no matter what. I have been trying to tell Natsai this, but her hatred for the young lady that Jerry brought in is so intense that she does not want to hear anything that even sounds like supporting her presence in our household.

She doesn't help either, Evelyn. Maybe it's America. Or maybe it's city life. She thinks asserting herself makes her something special. For some reason, she thinks Jerry considers her above us all, not least because she insisted on having her wing built away from us. What she doesn't know is that it suited us quite well. It makes her look like a lodger, a single mother with lodgings at the edge of the yard. That's the only revenge we laugh at her about.

As for me, I do not normally like to take sides, but my sympathies lie with Natsai. After all, she saved my marriage and brought me peace and happiness, and also triggered the re-opening of my ovaries. When I think about her, I am thankful that God allowed me to accept that Jerry brought her into our home. And, you know, he didn't need to ask me. My respect for him grew and I think that helped my relationship with Natsai, a truly humble woman who knows her place and has never tried to disrespect me at any point. Her only weakness is Evelyn and she thinks my attitude is too soft. As for me, I have seen a lot in my life and people like Evelyn are not the kinds of people to lose sleep over. It's a waste of time. Her personality and character were moulded outside the village and she cannot be changed.

Natsai calls her a slut. I think that's harsh. I know it is because of the story we heard about how she waylaid Jerry and deliberately fell pregnant so that she could have access to his money. I know that much to be true because Evelyn to me is like an open book. She forgets, or perhaps she doesn't know, that I've also lived in the city and am familiar with the life out there. I also accept, as far as she is concerned, Evelyn is doing what's right by her. It's sad but there is nothing we can do about how she conducts her business. She is a grown woman, even if she behaves sometimes like a teenager. As for me, I simply stay out of her way when I can – not least because I do not see what value she can add to my life. In any case, she's already created tension in the compound, made worse by her and Natsai's open antagonism towards each other. It's gone as far as Natsai claiming that Evelyn lives a double life. If it is true, then it will all come out; we were told that you cannot hide in a wrap that which has horns, and that when a drum beats too much, the skin will tear. As for me, I prefer to take all such talk as village gossip and concentrate on things I can manage, principal of which is to serve Jerry and help preserve his legacy for which he is respected in the entire village.

Our very first conversation is still very vivid in my mind. I recall how relieved I was that he came to talk to me, although I pretended to be casual about it. The truth is that I was having strange palpitations in class each time I looked at him and was not sure what was going on. Those palpitations disappeared from the time he said hello and only returned briefly when we met again at Mangwende Store after many years. We have not talked about it much but I found it difficult to have relationships when I was in nursing school, always wondering what had happened to him, why he had stopped writing. I even considered being a nun as I didn't believe there was any other man as good as Jerry. But God is God and we met again.

The stillbirth was a test, I now believe. A test for Jerry. A test for me. A test for our life together. A test for our real friendship. Jerry passed the test. As for me, I almost failed it. Jerry helped me pass it when he brought Natsai in. It's a strange solution, but it worked wonders for my mental health. I don't know how many women in polygamous unions can say that without feeling remorseful or even bitter.

Jerry and I have an understanding. As for me, I was very upset, of course, when Evelyn came in unannounced, and I almost lost it. Natsai was even more hysterical, and Jerry reacted very badly, but he had no right to threaten us like that when he was the one who provoked us. One day, after his threats, I found time to interrogate Jerry when he spent the night in my bedroom and, on reflection, I understood his explanation, although that doesn't mean I excused it. I understood. There is a difference.

When I thought about it later, I could only smile at Evelyn's deviousness. For the briefest of times, I wondered if, given similar circumstances and Jerry's stature, I could be driven to doing the same. It didn't work. It doesn't add up. She's a totally different character, young, impetuous, spontaneous and totally egocentric. I wonder if she will last here.

As for me, Jerry has demonstrated time and time again where I stand in his life. He is me, and I am him. I am the first wife, his one true friend, and I am not going anywhere, as long as we both shall live. I love Jerry. He loves me. We love each other. And that's all that matters.

THE WIDOW... AND A PHOTOGRAPH

SHE sat in the corner of the room. This was the custom and tradition expected of the newly bereaved widow, flanked left and right by the closest female relatives – perhaps sisters, the mother, or aunt – and surrounded in the room by a motley crew of appropriately sad-looking women. These expressions, too, were deliberately employed to send out the message of solidarity in grief: *you are not alone, for we mourn with you.*

Ruvarashe was thirty years old and had celebrated her birthday over dinner with her husband, best friend and best friend's boyfriend only a week before, the four of them. She was one of those fair-faced, even-toned girl-next-door types; easy going, ready smile and polite to a fault. She hated makeup and wore none. Her jet-black hair had grown into thick shiny dreadlocks which, for the moment, were covered by a multi-flowered *doek*. Her legs, firm and well-rounded when in sight, were right now hidden behind her, almost covered by a neat *chitenge* wrap skirt. Everyone thought she was well-named, because her name translated to God's Flower. Her face bloomed when she smiled, showing off an even set of very white teeth with a tiny gap between her top incisors and denting the cheeks with just a tiny hint of a reluctant dimple.

From across the room, Thandi shot her friend stolen glances. Today was the second day since Eric's sudden death and yet Thandi was still to see a single tear on Ruva's face. Thandi had been to many funerals and she was not one to make uninformed, negative conclusions about such behaviour. She was concerned because she knew how much Ruva and Eric loved each other and this seeming absence of emotion on her friend's part was a cause for worry, unless... She shook her head to dismiss an unwelcome thought. She lifted her eyes again and looked across the room. She let out a slow, gentle sigh of helplessness. Ruva was still motionless, staring at some space without blinking. She had not looked at Thandi once, and had averted her eyes when she consoled her.

Ruvarashe hung her head. No one knew what she was thinking at that moment. She was the object of pity, of sympathy and, at least for now, everyone wanted to do right by her.

A high-pitched wail rose above the singing, piercing the early evening air and shutting everyone up completely. Its owner was a slender, dark woman of average height who walked-staggered into the yard, seemingly oblivious to the attention she was attracting. As she got closer to the door, she added curses, pleas and complaints to the Creator, asking why he would do such a thing. After an appropriate amount of time, several women who were near the entrance, and some who had been at the cooking place at the back of the house and had come to see the spectacle, all joined her in the wailing and the din became an indescribable cacophony of discordant orchestra, akin to that of harmonica clashing with flute and cymbals.

Once inside the house, the woman increased her volume upon catching sight of Ruva and staggered hurriedly towards her, chattering incessantly. Ruva hugged her and, this time, the tears welled up in her eyes. Thandi thought this was more from the induced emotion than Ruva's own inner sensations. By now, everyone was sniffling and wiping away the spontaneous tears that were triggered by the woman's highly charged grief.

Her name was Barbara, and she was Eric's older sister. She was known to everyone as Babbu or Aunty Babbu and was Eric's only surviving sibling. There had been four of them in the family, but the twins had died in a freak accident at the family home, when a drunk driver crashed through the wall of their backyard where they were playing, imitating a wrestling match they had watched on television. He hit both of them and they died in hospital a few hours later, minutes after each other. Life in the family was never the same afterwards. The twins had been the family's source of pride and joy and had shown early signs of wit and intelligence. Their father went into severe depression and lost his job because his bouts of mental illness made him unproductive. They found their mother sprawled on the floor barely a week after his burial, the victim of a sudden fatal heart attack, said the pathologists.

Babbu at that time had barely turned twenty and had just started college. Eric was sixteen. The year they died, the twins were turning thirteen. Babbu made it her duty to look after her younger brother, interrupting her international relations studies to work as a temporary teacher so she could see him through his last years of high school. He never forgot this act of selflessness, and when he graduated as a civil engineer, he made sure he repaid his sister by helping her finish where she left off in school. The bond between them was unbreakable and she was all he could talk about when he met Ruva.

They met at a quiz show at the local university campus. Eric had gone to the show out of curiosity, finding himself without anything to do on a warm Friday night. The classmate he usually hung around with had gone home for the weekend. Eric was fascinated by the smiling girl in the pink dress and neatly combed Afro, who seemed to know everything about everything, whether it was mathematics, science, geography, history or literature.

"She's brilliant, isn't she?" a singsong voice said beside him. The voice belonged to Thandi. Eric discovered he had been smiling and nodding, sometimes even clapping like a cheerleader when Ruva got yet another answer right.

He and Thandi introduced each other and, within minutes, were chatting like old friends. Thandi brought Ruva to him when the show was over. A food and drinks stall had been set up and he got them all burgers and fizzy drinks. Thandi did most of the talking and Ruva, all the giggling. She was trying hard and failing just as much to take her eyes off Eric, who kept catching her at it and smiling back disarmingly. Eric learnt from Thandi that Ruva and her had agreed to study Pharmacy when they left high school.

A week later, Eric met Musa, Thandi's boyfriend. So began a close friendship that lasted throughout their college years and beyond. Ruva and Thandi loved the outdoors, which suited Eric fine. Every other weekend, they took drives into the countryside. Sometimes Musa came along, but most times Eric was alone with the two best friends. It seemed Musa had other passions that took him out of town a lot.

When they got married some two years after graduation, Thandi and Musa were the key witnesses. Thandi and Musa maintained their relationship but, for some reason, never got married despite their friends' urging. In time, it ceased to be an issue, turning instead into the butt of jokes between the two couples.

Ruva was three months pregnant when Eric died. They had been married for three and a half years and were living in a modest three-bedroom house that they rented in a middle-class location just outside the city favoured by young couples.

His postmortem revealed Eric had died of a sudden heart attack, just like his mother. There was no explanation for it and the pathologist, looking into Ruva's eyes, simply said that such things happen. He had not been sick, nor did he have any prior medical challenges. On the contrary, as Ruva herself told the police who came to collect the body, Eric had an active lifestyle. While he wasn't a teetotaller, he only drank for company and did not keep alcohol in the house. He liked to play soccer during weekends at the local sports club and they jogged together every morning to keep fit.

She had gone to sleep earlier the previous night, leaving him watching a late football game, she disclosed to the police. He was still sitting there when she got up and found he had not come to bed around three in the morning. He was staring sightlessly at the screen, the television remote control held loosely in his hand. His face, she said, looked like he had been surprised by something because he was open-mouthed. She called him first before she shook him, and that was when the remote control dropped out of his hand. And that is how the police found him when they arrived: open-mouthed, hand hanging at his side, his body half-slid off the sofa. The only thing Ruva said she touched were his eyes, which she had closed. When a policewoman asked about the small dribble of what appeared to be froth at the left corner of his mouth, Ruva had wiped it off swiftly with her handkerchief, saying casually that it had been worse when she closed his eyes. The policewoman stared at her for a while, frowned a little and decided not to prod further. Her partner may as well have noticed nothing throughout, focusing on taking notes, directing the photographer and watching the forensics team.

Babbu was inconsolable. She lamented the fact that she was now on her own and wondered why God was punishing her so. Was it not enough that he had taken her parents and little siblings? Now he had come and taken the only person that mattered to her, her last

treasure in life. What kind of God was he, that he could
be so cruel? It took the intervention of Ruva to get her to
eat anything. All the relatives and friends had failed and
eventually given up. At the burial, Ruva and Thandi
sandwiched her and held her firmly in the crooks of their
arms, lest she harm herself. It would be the last time
Ruva and her friend did anything together and, even
then, no words were exchanged.

Babbu stayed with Ruva for a month and a week after
her brother's death. There were memorial rituals to
perform, including the obligatory distributing of the
deceased's clothes amongst relatives. Ruva did not
recognise many of the relatives. She noted, however, that
a sizeable number walked around the house, from room
to room as if inspecting it and smiled when she
overheard a so-called aunt saying to someone in a failed
whisper, "No, I hear it's a rented house, so nothing
doing…"

They all left immediately after the clothes'
distribution, most of the suits and men's clothes going to
uncles and cousins that Ruva didn't know. Eric hardly
ever mentioned them and only talked about his big
sister, or the departed twins and his parents. It mattered
little – she had no use for the clothes anyway.

Babbu had mellowed somewhat and could now have
decent conversations with her sister-in-law. Ruva
couldn't help noticing how, sometimes, she caught
Babbu regarding her silently, chewing her lower lip or
the nail of her little finger. Caught like this, Babbu
would not look away guiltily but smile at her.

"I hope it's a boy," she said after dinner one evening,
smiling at Ruva's bulge.

"It is, *tete*," Ruva confirmed, returning the smile and involuntarily rubbing her belly.

There was some silence. "You and Eric…"

Ruva looked at her, but Babbu did not finish. Instead, she looked out the window, sighing and biting her lower lip.

Ruva tilted her head questioningly. "What is it, *tete?*"

Babbu looked at her for a while.

"After the distribution of the clothes," she said finally, "I went through the pockets of the leather jacket that I got for *Sekuru* back in the village. I found a photograph."

"A photograph, *tete?*"

In answer, Babbu reached for her handbag, which she had placed beside her on the sofa. She took out the photograph, and looked at it for a while before silently passing it to her sister-in-law.

Ruva looked at it. Her face was almost expressionless when she handed it back. But Babbu was looking at her intently and thought she detected a frown that disappeared almost as quickly as it had come.

"Do you know what it was doing in his jacket pocket?"

"I have no idea, *tete,*" she said, perhaps too quickly. "Maybe he meant to give it to me and forgot."

"Hmm." After a considered pause, Babbu asked, "Was everything ok between you? I mean, you and my brother. Why would…"

"We were fine, *tete*. We were fine. I don't think you should read too much into that. It's just a photograph. We were fine."

"Well, why did you give it back to me then? I would expect you to take it to her, confront her, ask her what it was doing in your man's jacket pocket. That's what I would do. That's what *I* would do!"

"*Tete*," Ruva said as calmly and softly as she could, "Eric and I loved each other. We were the best of friends. Ever since Thandi introduced us, I have never… we never…"

Babbu thought she heard Ruva choke on her friend's name. Tears welled up in her eyes. Presently she started sobbing and then crying outright. She quaked uncontrollably and her tears became rivulets that drenched her chest. So long did she cry, but Babbu only observed her like an artist would survey his prize sculpture. She did not make any move towards her but simply nodded. Suddenly, she pursed her lips, got up, picked up her handbag and left the room. She left the photograph where she had been sitting. Ruva continued to cry and, when she trudged off to bed, she continued to cry into the pillow and fell asleep crying. It was the most she had cried since her husband's death.

Her eyes were puffed when she woke up later than usual the next morning. She found Babbu in the kitchen, cleaning the dishes from last night.

"Good morning, *muroora*," she greeted in a flat voice.

"Good morning, *tete*," Ruva answered, her voice equally flat.

"I made breakfast. I've already had mine. Yours is in the warmer."

"Thank you, *tete*." Ruva got a glass and poured herself some drinking water.

She was drinking it slowly when Babbu walked towards her from the sink, drying her hands on a towel.

"I am leaving. Promise me that you will call him Eric

Junior."

Ruva nodded firmly. She put her glass on the counter slowly and regarded her sister-in-law, not fighting back the tears. She walked towards her, and they hugged in a tight, wordless embrace that lasted a full minute. They wiped each other's tears away and Babbu rubbed Ruva's shoulders. She shook her head slowly and walked away. Ruva leaned on the sink and cried again.

The taxi picked Babbu up an hour later. Ruva waved and stared for a long time at it and the space where it had driven out of sight. She rubbed her belly and went back into the house. Absently, she picked up the photograph that Babbu had left on her sofa, looked at it expressionlessly for a while then tore it into pieces and threw it into the fireplace. Photographs of her and Eric stared back at her as she passed through the living room and went into the bathroom to take a long hot bath.

***

Detective Inspector Samson Phiri said he was from the Homicide Division of the Criminal Investigations Department. He expressed condolences to Ruva on the death of her husband and asked her to repeat how Eric had died, if she didn't mind.

She minded very much. Five months had passed. She found his seeming sincerity disarming but was surprised that she was not irritated by it. She also wondered why he was alone. As far as she knew, police investigating details moved in twos or even threes. But she kept her curiosity to herself. She repeated what she had told the police who attended to her distress call. She spoke slowly.

DI Phiri nodded, taking a few notes and looking from her to some papers in the file he had brought with him. Occasionally he shot a sympathetic smile at her, shaking his head at appropriate intervals as she narrated her story. Occasionally, too, a frown crossed his brow, but he quickly extinguished it with the encouraging smile. He was struck by the way her narration was an almost faithful mirror of the statement she had given the police five months earlier as recorded in the file.

He asked the same question that Aunty Babbu had asked months earlier, whether there was any misunderstanding between her and Eric. Ruva said there was none, apart from the usual couples' tiffs over money and other petty things such as leaving drawers open, clothes lying around, squeezing the toothpaste tube in the centre, that kind of thing.

DI Phiri smiled knowingly and nodded. "How long were you married for?"

"Three, almost four years." She returned his smile.

"You loved him."

She smiled again. It was not a question. But she nodded.

He looked at his notes. He seemed to hesitate before asking his next question. Then he looked up and stared into her eyes.

"Does your friend, what's her name, um, this one…Thandiwe Mpala… does Thandiwe visit you often?"

"She was here yesterday," Ruva lied. He took interest in her clasped hands, uneasy under the detective's steady gaze. She and Thandi had not spoken since Eric's burial. Ruva had cut her off, had cut off all past acquaintances and blocked Thandi's line. The one time Thandi visited her physically, Ruva refused to open the door and Thandi stopped trying to talk to her not long after. Eventually, she and Musa broke up and Thandi left to work in Namibia. DI Phiri knew all this. He looked at Ruva long and hard, then smiled again and nodded.

"Yeah. Yeah. Sometimes us men do the strangest things," he said, sighing. The statement seemed out of place in his line of questioning. He closed his folder, got up abruptly and thrust out his free hand to shake hers and thank her for her time. Ruva was puzzled. She frowned as she shook DI Phiri's hand. She opened her mouth as if to say something.

"Have a good day, my sister," he said, interrupting her to silence. He walked towards the door, where he stopped and looked back at a still frowning, open-mouthed Ruva.

He smiled at her belly. "I hope it's a boy," he said, and closed the door softly.

THE THWARTED PLAN

ON one clear, blue skied Saturday morning in September, when everything was still and calm following a very windy week, Observer Gwatiringa thought of a plan. It was a plan for revenge. He told himself it was no longer the time to keep quiet and do nothing, as if he was immune to hurt. Just this once, Observer decided, just this once he needed to show that he was made of sterner stuff than he was given credit for. This was important.

First, though, he needed to do some deep thinking. Somewhere quiet, where he would be all alone without any interruption, without any distractions. There, he could tease out his plan and critique it, go over it as many times as he needed to.

Observer knew just the place. He packed his aluminium-lined cooler bag with enough water to last him the day and, in a side pocket, threw in a packet of roasted peanuts and biltong from game meat that his uncle had brought from his farm. An orange and an apple completed the tuck, and Observer was good to go. He closed and locked the doors of his sparsely furnished apartment, took one look around to make sure everything, including the windows, was secured, and drove his car out of the carport, one of many allocated to tenants at the block of double-story apartments.

He had not even made it to the gate. The vehicle felt heavy as he reversed out of the carport and drove forward a little. Observer got out and confirmed his fears: puncture, and – unknown to him yet on this day – the first sign of trouble.

Observer sighed and cursed in frustration. It took him just over half an hour to replace the offending tyre because a madman had secured the wheel nuts so tight that he had to stand on the spanner to make them come off. He lost valuable time doing that. He washed his hands at the outside tap and was soon on his way. Gradually his mood improved, and he put on some smooth Afro-jazz music to suit. Just outside the city limits, he turned into a shopping centre parking area on a whim. He had decided a bottle of wine might help with the thinking.

There were people crowding around his car when he got out of the supermarket. Sign of trouble number two. Observer quickened his pace, his mind a whirl of anxiety and foreboding.

People were shouting all at once. Observer forced his way through the crowd and, when it was established that he was the driver they were waiting for, they made way for him.

"*Mota yakwesherwa mudhara!*"

"She wanted to drive off! We stopped her!"

"*Ngaarohwe! Ngaarohwe!*"

"Unlicensed drivers are a problem!"

"Yes, this is the problem with buying licenses instead of doing proper lessons."

"*Aiwa,* let them talk, this is a small matter!"

"*Ehe*, let them talk and agree. It's just a scratch that…"

"*Iwe!* Is that what you call a scratch? This is a Beemer my friend."

"People that don't have cars are a problem!"

"Who doesn't have a car? Talk about what you know my friend!"

"Stop calling me 'friend'. You're not my friend, my friend!"

Laughter.

In between, Observer was able to see that a deep gash had neatly put a new, unsolicited design on the whole passenger side of his car, from just under the front door handle right through to almost the rear fender. The unhappy designer, such as she was, was standing outside the driver's door of a small, shiny blue, new-looking car which she had manoeuvred just out of the parking bay next to Observer's black monstrosity. Mobbed and clearly frightened out of her wits, she was desperately trying to explain herself, but no one was listening.

"You wanted to run away!"

"No, please, understand me, please, please, I beg you…"

"There's nothing you are saying!"

"Please, *kani*…"

"*Mahure munonetsa!*" And, at this, she consciously tried to pull down her little skirt, but it stubbornly stood firm, having nowhere more to go.

"Leave her alone, guys, she was just frightened that she had scratched someone's…" a middle-aged man tried to reason, but he only managed to attract the ire of the crowd, mostly the men.

"*Haa, iwe mudhara iwe!* Shut up! Don't try to seek favours."

"*Anakirwa ne* mini skirt!"

"That's not a mini skirt. That's a large belt!"

More laughter.

Observer knelt to feel the damage to his car and confirmed that it was bad and would be costly to repair. When he got up, he almost bumped into the author of the problem. She was in tears and shaking, her frame in a hump as if she was trying to sink into herself, her hands clasped together. She was wide-eyed with fright, perhaps thinking the mob would set upon her, or Observer himself would start pummelling her sorry face.

"I'm so sorry *bhudhi*, I'm so very sorry," she managed to say between sobs. "It's my sister's car and I…I…I panicked!"

"*Musavharwe blaz!* Crocodile tears *idzo!*" someone shouted.

Observer just looked at her, as if stunned. Which he was. She was a beauty, and the crying seemed to make her even more beautiful. A sudden wave of sympathy and something else he couldn't explain overwhelmed him. He found himself taking out a clean handkerchief from his pocket and extending it to her.

It was her turn to be stunned. She hesitated before she took it and wiped her tears off in a very crude, unladylike manner. *Lucky that she doesn't have powder and those other things on her face that women paint themselves with*, Observer thought. He looked at the ground, to hide the smile that was invading his face as he thought a private thought. When he looked up again, she still had the same pleading, desperate look.

He reached for his handkerchief, and she handed it back. She was frowning. Observer still hadn't said anything. Now he turned to the mob and said in an even but commanding tone that surprised even himself, "May you please leave us. I must talk to this lady and sort this problem out. Thank you for stopping her. Thank you. Thank you. Now leave us, please."

They moved away but did not go too far. Observer picked up some unsavoury murmurings but decided to ignore them. A truckload of police officers arrived and managed to shoo them a longer distance farther. One of the policemen jumped out and approached Observer and the girl.

"What seems to be the problem here?"

"Morning officer. She scratched my vehicle while driving out, so…"

"May I see your licenses, please?"

The girl cringed in fright. Observer noted this and quickly spoke out, all the while making slow, feigned movements to make the policeman believe he was reaching for the license in his wallet.

"No need, officer. We're good. It's not too bad, we were just about to conclude our agreement."

The officer looked from one to the other. Two more

officers came and wanted to know what was happening.

"Minor accident. He says they have agreed."

"Ah, well, if they have agreed then we are not needed here. Let's go."

They left. They had some vendors to shepherd out of the CBD and had been attracted to this side show by the mob, otherwise it was just a distraction.

She was blabbering some thank you's as they drove off. This time Observer did not hide his smile. The crowd saw her nodding furiously, her hands still clasped together in a sign of penance, curtsying continuously. The tears flowed again, but this time Observer did not offer his hanky. She wiped them off with the back of her hand. The crowd witnessed the exchange of phone numbers, Observer opening the door of her car and standing there to watch her as she drove off.

A sudden loud cheer and clapping went up from the mob as Observer smiled and waved at the receding car.

"*Gaffa! Gaffa! Gaffa!*" they cheered.

He got into his car, placed his paper bag onto the passenger seat and gently reversed out and drove off. The cheers were still ringing in his ears as he pulled away and, when he looked in the mirror, a few men were chasing his car, whistling and applauding. Observer laughed this time and shook his head at the unexpected turn of events.

There was an uprooted gum tree across the road when Observer took the dusty pathway branching off to the river. Sign of trouble number three. It must have been pulled up by the heavy wind the previous day or night. But, Observer thought doubtfully, do gum trees uproot that easily? He got out of the car and walked slowly towards it. There was no sign of anyone else around, or so it seemed, until he got closer. There were men in dirty, oily, tattered overalls standing on the other side. They had been cut off from view by the huge branches and leaves.

"When did this tree fall?" he shouted across at them.

"Last night!" one shouted back.

Another asked, "You want to pass, boss?"

Observer didn't answer. It wasn't a very clever question.

"We will get it out of the way for you, our boss," a third one said.

Observer nodded and watched them getting ready before walking slowly back to his car, where he sat with the door open, thinking what a testing day it had been so far. They hacked away with their axes for quite a while, until they had cut off enough of the tree to allow them to pull away the barrier.

"We are done, boss, you may pass," one of the men announced. He didn't seem to be out of breath, although he was sweating. "You are the first one here."

Observer got out of the car to look. They approached him in a line, like soldiers in formation. He watched them holding their axes loosely, strange smiles on their faces. There were six of them. They had unbuttoned the tops of their overalls, and some had tied the sleeves at the waistline, chests and six-packs glistening with sweat from the exertion in the afternoon sun. Observer nodded at them slowly, looking from one to the other and showing not the least bit of emotion. What a bunch of ugly renegades, he thought. He also noted that they were effectively blocking his passage, even if they invited him to proceed.

"Money for drink, boss," a particularly dark, heavy-set man said in a thick voice from somewhere to Observer's left. He grinned and displayed a set of yellow teeth. Three of the teeth were missing, giving him the rather comical yet frightening mark of the type that gets high on violence. Observer smiled.

He held up his left hand to signal "wait-a-moment" and took out his wallet. Slowly, he moved to the left of the line, handing each one of them a five-dollar note until he reached the other end. He thanked his lucky stars that the supermarket had given him that kind of change.

"*Mbinga!*" the ragged, yellow-toothed man shouted.

"*Mbinga-a-a!*" his comrades responded, axes held high, and they parted to allow him to drive through. They would be able to buy each other two rounds or more of opaque beer at the local speakeasy and get home suitably drunk.

The drive from Observer's apartment to this part of the river would normally take him just twenty minutes, but Observer found he had taken more than two hours now between the tyre puncture, the incident with the almost hit-and-run girl and the fallen gum tree. He drove round to his favourite spot, behind a forest of gum trees and out onto a space that suddenly opened to reveal a paradise-imbued part of the river that was hidden from view.

Observer reflected on the three incidents, shook his head and tried to push them out of his head. He needed to focus and turn his mind to his plan.

Too many things had happened in too short a space

of time. Observer went round to the boot of his car and took out a mat that he kept there specially for occasions when he had to picnic. He laid it out on the ground near the car and sat, using the vehicle's body as his backrest. He was finding it difficult to concentrate, so he went back to the boot and took out his cooler bag, opened the passenger door and took out the wine bottle and tumbler he had bought at the supermarket.

Soon, he was alternately popping nuts into his mouth and chewing on his biltong, occasionally taking a sip of wine, alternating that too with the water. He watched the river and the crystals of light dancing on its surface. It was amazing that the water here was un-muddied and clear, unlike the rest of the river, which threatened to be choked by hyacinth and silt. When he stood up, he could see the variety of fish swimming happily up and down, safe from fishermen. Observer was not a fish eater nor was he interested in fishing, although he liked to watch them in their natural habitat, wondering what they were thinking, if they thought anything. He watched the fireflies and the butterflies and the dragon flies – they called them "helicopters" when he was a young boy – and he marvelled at the tiny, blue-chested grey birds that could perch on flimsy grass stalks, telling himself, not for the first time, that he needed to learn the names of birds if he was to enjoy the outdoors more. He regretted having left his camera at home.

"Go away!" one of the other birds now said to him from the safety of a tree branch somewhere above and was echoed by others not far away.

Observer smiled and said out loud, "I'm not going anywhere!" He laughed and enjoyed his private moment of freedom, out here in the natural wild, all on his own.

He smiled even more as his mind went back to Prisca, the girl who had scratched his car. What a way to meet! He was sure they would meet again but there was no question of asking her to repair the damage. She looked like she wasn't yet a person of means.

There was a rustling sound and Observer sat up. Sign of trouble number four. He looked around. Nothing. He pricked his ears and wished there was some way to silence the chirping and tweeting birds, the whistling crickets and the singing insects. There. The rustling sound came again. Observer got up and closed the door of his car after peering inside. He tiptoed to the other side and was about to laugh at the sight of a large bullfrog bobbing its huge eyes restlessly from its perch upon a rust-coloured rock where it had just launched itself, except… Observer leapt back in fright as the snake struck at precisely that moment, paralysing the frog immediately. When he gathered the courage to look again, it was to see the tail of the slimy, decorous reptile disappearing into the thick foliage on the other side. Bullfrog was gone, turned into a live, raw snack just like that.

Observer told himself he had had enough drama for one day. He packed his stuff and drove out of there with single-minded resolve. Plans will have to wait. In any case, when has revenge ever benefited anyone? One cannot expect to be loved by everyone as if they are food. You can be as good a person as possible and still find people who cannot stand the sight of you. And for no reason too – if everything must have a reason. Let those with personal vendettas and agendas and plots and schemes vendetta their lives away, if it made them feel better.

Observer made himself a light meal when he got home, took a cold shower and made a call to Prisca, ostensibly to check if she had got home fine. A new, attainable plan started to unravel, and Observer slept with a happy face that night and dreamt a happy dream.

JOSPHAT'S WELL

JOSPHAT shielded his eyes but still needed to squint, because the brightness of the sun was too intense. It was mid-morning, but he was already sweating heavily. However, the sun in his eyes, the sweating and the sweltering heat were the least of Josphat's worries. He stooped to prise open the lid covering the well at the corner of his yard. This had become a daily routine, the checking of the water in the well. And his worst fears were confirmed when he dipped in the long stick that he used as a gauge: it was drying up fast and up to now, Josphat had not been able to think of any way to conserve the little that was left.

In the end, he emptied a drum in which he had stored some maize grain and used a bucket and rope to scoop up the water and into the drum. It took him just less than an hour and when he was done, he carefully tied plastic sheeting around the mouth of the drum using a lengthy strip of bark from the lot that he had harvested in the forest and placed the drum's lid on top.

The maize grain he put in sacks and secured them in a corner of the granary where, for good measure and security, he pulled an old cupboard in front of his treasure so that it was not immediately visible to an errant visitor. He also threw some old items of furniture and dysfunctional implements around the area so that it looked like another ordinary junk corner. In tough times, hunger can turn the most upright man into a daring criminal. It is best, therefore, to hide temptation from sight.

Josphat stood at the entrance of the granary and critically surveyed his handiwork. He wiped his brow and walked back to the well, where he tilted and wheeled his precious drum to the back of the granary, out of sight.

"*Baba a-Mimi!*" his wife called from one of the huts and Josphat found himself smacking his teeth in irritation. He did not answer, but instead, started walking in the direction of the voice, with the call being made repeatedly.

She was in the kitchen, smoke billowing out characteristically. She smiled at him warmly and he melted. She had that effect on him.

"What are you doing?" she asked, neither needing nor waiting for a response. "I made some porridge."

He sat on the bench, a permanent fixture of raised solid clay built around the hut, against the wall. Shelving on the walls was made the same way, and his wife, quite the decorative artist in her own right, had neatly arranged her colourfully painted clay pots and other utensils. Only the tea pot and teacups were steel, presents from Josphat's brother in the city.

She handed him a plate filled with a wooden spoon and piping hot porridge made from sorghum grain. Josphat took a scoop to his mouth and immediately regretted it.

The spectacle of him sucking air into his mouth in an attempt to cool his burnt tongue and cheeks sent his wife into a fit of laughter.

"But you know I always serve my porridge hot, Baba a-Mimi!" she laughed. "You should be careful."

Josphat was looking for an appropriate response, but little Mimi, playing on the reed mat in the corner across the room, joined her mother and giggled excitedly although she had no idea what the joke was. Once more, Josphat melted and grinned at the girl.

"So, you too think this is funny, eh?"

Mimi giggled again as Josphat blew into the porridge and resumed eating, more slowly and carefully this time.

His wife watched him as he ate, a smile on her face. She allowed her mind to wander once again, back to the time when this man, then a mere seventeen-year-old boy, had swept her off her feet. He was coming from foraging for edible maggots in the hills of the forest which, when deep fried by an expert, made for a sumptuous, juicy protein snack or even a relish. Josphat had a bagful of them, still alive and wriggling over and around each other. She was returning from fetching firewood from another end of the same forest. They met where the paths met to resume as the single pathway that linked the village to the forest.

She saw him trying to subtly size her up. For his part, Josphat was feeling funny inside. He had not seen anything like this. She was dressed simply, in a long frock that went way past her knees. Under her *doek*, strands of dark hair showed she could have long, almost straight hair if she wanted. Hers was the kind of light complexion that people said stemmed from associations with visiting Portuguese traders who made forays into the country from neighbouring Mozambique. In Zimbabwe, just as in Mozambique, they fraternised with the locals, resulting in new genetic combinations that were passed onto subsequent generations. Josphat had no interest in such stories. All he could see was how alluring that copper-cum-chocolate colour looked .

"I know you," Josphat accused. "You are Mudhara Mamutse's daughter."

She stared at him without expression. Then, she made a smacking sound with her tongue and smirked, "Is that a crime?"

The answer-question brought a huge smile on Josphat's face. The Mamutse girls were well known in the village, on account of their outstanding beauty. It was said of their mother that she was descended from the Portuguese foreigners. Josphat had only seen them from a distance but took no more than an amused interest. This one, though, this one he had never seen.

"Here, let me help you," he said and, before she knew what was happening, he had dislodged the burden on her head and transferred it to his left shoulder.

"I am Josphat," he offered, interrupting any protest she was about to make. She now stood akimbo, face pouting and ready to spew whatever venom she could make up at that moment. Instead, she found herself regarding him anew and noticed that she had not really *noticed* him. She, too, had not seen this boy before, but immediately liked his big bright eyes and knotted hair. The nose and lips were a little too large, though. And he was a shade too dark as well. But he looked tall and athletic, and had an easy smile. There passed some seconds while they stared at each other. And then she smiled and scoffed.

"Josphat what?"

Josphat's smile had not left his face. "Josphat Taremekedzwa Anotida Samson Musarara."

"Eew, so many names for one person! How do they fit on a birth?"

She meant a birth certificate. Like everyone else, she pronounced it "bethy". Josphat laughed.

"You have not told me yours."

"But you said you know me."

"Just what I have been told, that you're Mudhara Mamutse's daughter. They didn't tell me the actual name."

"Who? And why were they telling you?"

"The boys at the school. I just heard them talking and…"

"Ah. I didn't know boys gossip as well."

Josphat wasn't expecting this, and he gaped at her.

"My name is Chipo Tatenda Mamutse. Please close your mouth. Flies will enter."

Chipo smiled more broadly at the memory, recalling how fast her heart was beating even as she turned her back to him and started to walk confidently along the pathway. She could hear his footsteps and almost feel his breath as he walked after her. She had not known there was such a boy in the village, and she liked him almost instantly. Could that be possible? At fifteen, she had thought she already understood what love was even though she had not personally experienced it herself. Could that have been the first time?

"What's making you smile like that, mother of my child?" Josphat couldn't help smiling as he watched his wife's soft, relaxed face. He was amazed at how she'd not lost her beauty all these years after their marriage, and a two-year-old girl to consummate the union. It was a fair and natural face, with not a zit in sight. Her hair was plaited in neat cornrows, courtesy of one of her sisters who was the village specialist in such hairdressing, and the smile never seemed to leave her face. Josphat felt blessed and prayed another silent prayer of gratitude for his fortune. Since that day when they chanced upon each other as teenagers, not a harsh word had passed between them. Josphat recalled that, even when they felt irritated by each other's little bad habits, the ties that bound them ensured that such things were treated as inconsequential as they were.

They were the talk of the village from the time their "friendship" became public knowledge at the mission school where both took their secondary school studies. When the popular song was released about a similar legendary affair south of the country, the people in their village told anyone that cared to listen that they, too, had their own Solo and Mutsai lovebirds. The song was played endlessly at the village shopping centre and there were not a few that feared that the needle might bore a hole the size of the one in the centre of the vinyl plate and the song would be heard no more. The optimists would laugh and say, quite reasonably, that there were so many record players and gramophones that when one shut down, another would simply take its place.

"I have news for you, Ba-Mimi," Chipo said in her lilting voice.

Josphat's heart skipped a beat. He finished the last of his porridge and wiped the plate with two fingers, which he proceeded to lick. To dry them, he rubbed them in his hair. It was one of those irritating habits that Chipo had never got used to, but she ignored it and took the plate from him, placing it beside her for washing later with the other dishes.

"I think Mimi is going to have a brother," she said, watching him intently and trying hard to keep the excitement out of her voice.

He stared at her, open-mouthed. She tilted her head at him as he gaped at her stomach. She rubbed it instinctively in a circular motion. Josphat rose slowly, knelt on both knees and crawled towards her like an animal stalking prey, mouth still open.

"C-C-Close, close your m-mouth, Joe," she said as he got closer, her voice suddenly a bare trembling whisper. She was breathing heavily, as she always did when he approached her like this.

"The flies will enter," he whispered back as he eased himself beside her. He removed her hand from her belly and rubbed it gently in the same slow circular motion. He adjusted his seating to allow himself to lay his head on the belly. Chipo adjusted herself too, to assist him. Mimi went very quiet, perhaps sensing the mood. After a few seconds staring at them, she whimpered once, lay down and promptly fell asleep. Watching her, the couple laughed quietly.

"I cannot feel or hear him," Josphat pronounced in a

low voice after a while.

"He is a quiet gentleman, like his father."

Josphat looked up at her face. He smiled and said, "Maybe he doesn't have ears to hear with yet. Let's give him some…"

"Aah, Josphat…" Chipo whispered weakly in complete submission, as her husband's hands wrapped her up in a gentle but firm embrace.

***

Josphat used his land well and never wanted for anything. Maize, groundnuts, pumpkins, sorghum, sweet potatoes, roundnuts… All thrived on the plot of land that his father had parcelled out to him when he cut up his larger plot for his sons. Where one brother sold his and left for the city and the other was inconsistent – good one season, fallow the next – Josphat's land was the envy of the community. He was good with his hands and his compound was among the neatest, with solid structures. He had a good wife, too, because she supported him well in everything he did. Mbuya Kiri, Josphat's father's mother, had moved heaven and earth to ensure that her son found enough cattle for the bride that her grandson had decided to bring home. They had prayed from the time it became clear that nothing in the village could separate the two. Besides, the Mamutse girls were prize brides that families wished for their sons. Despite being the rich man of the community, with his grinding mill, fuel and mechanics garage, two shops – one for hardware and farm equipment and the other for groceries – Mudhara Mamutse raised his four sons and four daughters to be respectful and humble. Apart from Chipo and one sister, however, when they grew up, they all moved to jobs and life in the city and overseas, where they raised their own families.

But right now, Josphat's fields were a pathetic sight. All the other fields in the village were the same, or worse. The drought had set in the previous season. When it became clear that no rain was coming, the village elders called for a community meeting where it was agreed that Mwari be approached through prayer, entreating Him to have pity on them and to forgive whatever offense had angered Him so. This was an important assignment that would be led by the village's spirit mediums who knew how to communicate with Mwari through *vadzimu*, spirits of long-gone ancestors whose job it was to continue to look after the families from whom they had departed physically. Had they forsaken them? Why? Was Mwari angry? Had someone committed some transgression that required punishing the whole village with the harshest of punishments – hunger? Bones had been thrown, all-night vigils kept, visits to the mountains and all the secret sacred places conducted, all to no avail. The skies remained clear, sometimes with not even a cloud in sight. The sun continued to burn its harshest. Evil had visited the Earth, and the dry ground started cracking. The Earth was scorched, and the Devil was enjoying himself.

The year was 1992. The drying genesis had taken almost a good two years to manifest. After the crops wilted and died, the animals started following. Hunger stalked the land and thousands of cattle dropped where they stood, too emaciated to get up. Rivers, dams, wells and all other water sources simply dried up, and the desolation carried itself into people's bodies, cracking up minds and sucking out any mental resolve there may have been.

From the city, Josphat's brother reported that the government was saying there were virtually no harvests throughout the country. He said the whole country had only two days' supply of food left and had no choice but to turn to neighbours and other countries outside the continent to bring food. But whatever food came was consumed on arrival, such was the level of need. Josphat's brother said in any case, this drought also affected the neighbouring countries who, with the best goodwill, could only spare so much from their food reserves because they needed to look after their own people and had started importing as well. The country deteriorated from food surplus to net food importer almost overnight. Josphat's brother accused the government of neglect and questioned their capacity for disaster preparedness.

It was language Josphat did not understand and cared little for. It seemed misplaced, idle talk in the face of what he and the other villagers were going through. But this was the problem with city people… always finding time for useless conversations when lives were at stake. The fact was there had been no rain, and hunger stalked the land – that was the reality. Who caused it, how they caused it, and any other questions were not going to change the situation. Did Mukoma want government to make the rain fall?

The food aid machine got into motion. Every week, Josphat's village welcomed truckloads of food, but they only offloaded what was felt met basic food requirements for the village community and moved on to the next villages with the rest. When their share was distributed, it was far too little and only lasted a few days, then they would have to wait for the next visit.

The drought had been predicted by the forecasters of such things, but very few people had thought it would last this long. Many thought that it was nothing the normal prayers for rain would not be able to sort out. But as it continued, first with one season and then the next, the prayers became more fervent and desperate. In the second dry season, Josphat took advantage of the little rains that fell to dig a well in his compound and capture some rainwater into a drum that he had placed on stilts in an open space behind his hut.

But that was last year. Today, his well was on the verge of drying completely. At the rate the sun was sucking the moisture out of any life left, things did not look too good. Already he had used up the water from his drum and used it to store what little grain he had managed to salvage from his fields. It was this same drum he had decided to empty and fill with the last of the water from the well, reasoning that it stood a better chance of lasting longer in a container than in the fast-drying ground.

***

Mimi stirred. In a moment, she was awake and immediately started crying. It woke Josphat too and he cursed himself for sleeping in the daytime. His wife was nowhere in sight and, realising his nakedness, Josphat quickly pulled on his shorts, guiltily looking at the baby who had started to crawl towards him. He picked her up and started rocking her, humming the tune that he had heard the child's mother singing. Little Mimi must have hated his version. Her crying graduated to wailing in full song and Josphat almost threw her down in exasperation and fright.

Chipo's shadow filled the doorway. She shook her head and gently prised her daughter away. Mimi quietened immediately, tugging at her mother's chest and succeeding in undoing a button on her blouse. A breast popped out as mother dutifully complied and little Mimi cupped her little hands and lips around it. She sucked hungrily. It was as if she knew she would be taken off it soon.

Chipo looked at Josphat sitting cross-legged, glaring at her and laughed softly. She shook her head again and teased, "Shall we say good morning?"

Josphat snorted and pushed himself up. "How long have I been sleeping? What's the time?"

Chipo made a show of looking outside and up. She seemed to be enjoying herself.

"Hmm, let me see. You were not sleeping. You died, but it looks like you're Lazarus and Jesus came. Time? It looks like all the cattle would have been coming home now, if that which finished all the goats had not eaten the cattle as well."

It was, indeed, late afternoon. Josphat strode purposefully to the back of the house and picked up his axe. Soon, Chipo heard the sharp thud, thud, of axe on wood as she took some time rocking Mimi. Presently, she shifted the baby to her back, and fastened her with a large towel. This allowed her to busy herself with preparing for the evening chores, consisting mainly of cooking for her family, making sure the mats in their sleeping hut were ready, the evening fire was going and everything that should be in its place was where it was supposed to be. She hummed a popular traditional tune as she set about her tasks, but deep down, she was as worried about the drought as her husband.

He was up at dawn the next morning and strode off in the direction of the fields. It seemed to Chipo a futile chore. There was nothing there, except evidence of desolation, hunger and the pain the hunger caused. Chipo recalled that, as the drought was setting in, she had agreed that they sell the few cattle they had been given by both sets of parents as wedding presents, to set them off on their new life as husband and wife. She was glad they had had that foresight, as reports were coming in of cattle dying every day in large numbers. Now the cattle kraal at the far end of their compound stood only as a stark reminder.

Chipo was a perpetual optimist and believed strongly in her husband's capacity to get his family out of any sticky situation. This was why you could never find her openly showing signs of worry. She preferred to count her blessings. Josphat and Mimi were big blessings as it was, and she considered herself the luckiest bride in the village. Ever since that day in the forest, Josphat had only ever had eyes for her, and she was thankful there was some positive conspiracy in the village to keep their relationship as it was, so that disruptors were quickly discouraged. The only thing that filled her with dread was the idea of living in the city. She had heard so many stories of lives upended when villagers ventured out there, and she wanted nothing to do with it. Thankfully, Josphat agreed with her on this, but… What if this drought changed his mind? Sometimes she detected pride in his voice when he spoke about his brother's experiences that he shared with them: cars, city lights, easy living, everyone minding their own business, no village gossip or interference. Of course, they would both laugh and say, "How can you live on your own, without anyone coming to borrow some mealie meal? Is that even a life?"

Out on the fields, Josphat was a worried man. He stood on a hill, from where he could see the vast expanse below. As he scanned and his eyes traversed the terrain from one end to another, the brow on his forehead grew more intense. Josphat stood for a long time, his shoulders sagging, defeated. To make matters worse, the wind had stopped blowing, and the clouds had left the sky, too scared to confront the force of the intense sun. Even the forest sounds had died – no crickets, no cicadas, no birds, nothing. For its turn, the sun burnt down mercilessly and Josphat thought, at this rate, it was going to create a fire somewhere that would co-conspire to obliterate everything in its path. The Devil was still enjoying himself.

Josphat started to walk down the other side of the hill when his resolve could not take the heat anymore. He headed for the *musasa* and *mutohwe* trees, to sit under their shade and think. There was much to think about, chief of which was how to stave off the hunger that was surely to come for his family, as it had many others in the village already. His brother in the city said news reports disclosed that millions were officially known to be affected, many children malnourished and the situation was very desperate. But try as he could with all the scary stories, he failed to convince Josphat to escape to the city where life was said to be better. Josphat would not even consider it.

He thought about this now, as he wearily deposited himself against the trunk of a tree and stretched one leg out in front of him, the other bent at the knee. He picked a twig and started to break it into small pieces that he would throw a distance away. He looked absent-mindedly at the last little piece in his hand, turning it around before putting it between his teeth. He chewed on it, rolling it from one side of his mouth to the other. Eventually, he spat it out and tried to think. But his mind wandered, with flashes of incoherent thoughts. He looked into the far distance again, but there was no future there that he could see. Everything was a smoky haze, desperately unwelcoming and energy-sapping. When a grass snake slithered past a little later, Josphat, in creeping drowsiness, only looked at it idly, and watched it with mild interest. Grass snakes could be quite colourful, were generally not dangerous, non-venomous and…

Josphat sat up suddenly. Grass snake! It seemed to momentarily stop and look at him, forked tongue flashing, before it set off again. He got up and started following it carefully, hoping not to scare it off into hiding.

His heart was beating fast. Could this even be possible? Could there be water somewhere close by? Everything had dried up and it just seemed improbable.

But then… what was this *thing* doing here? Growing up, his father had always told him these creatures played around places where there was water, sometimes in the water itself, because they fed on things that were found in water, such as frogs.

The snake slid into a thorn bush too thick for Josphat to follow. He stood there a while, contemplating what to do next. In the end, since he did not have any weapon or implement of any kind, he decided to go round the bush, but it was a long way round. By the time he got to the other side, the snake was nowhere in sight.

Josphat looked around desperately, but all he could see was dry grass and more thorn bushes. He looked at the ground, hoping to see even the snake's trail, but the earth was dry and cracked, and no moving thing could leave a trail there. He allowed himself a smile as he knelt and thought if anyone came by and asked him what he was doing, his answer that he was looking for a snake would cause all sorts of speculation, even fear. Only witches and medicine people hunted snakes, for rituals, antidotes and "black magic", otherwise everyone else steered clear of them, harmless or not. For some, the mere sight or mention of snakes gave them nightmares, and they would not sleep at night or dare to bask under tree shades.

Josphat shook his head in defeat and stood up, mopping sweat off his brow for the umpteenth time. He cupped his hand against his forehead to shield his eyes from the sun and slowly looked around, completing a full circle. He sighed and started to trudge back the way he had come, keeping his eye out for either the snake or perhaps a relative of it, if there was a habitat somewhere close by.

Not for the first time that day, Josphat stopped in his tracks and tilted his head, listening. While he had been walking around, the sounds of insects – sounds of the forest – had resumed, and he had not noticed because they were the most natural sounds that he had grown up subconsciously accepting as part of the forest.

Seconds passed. Then he heard it again. The unmistakable croak of Chura, the frog, was music to Josphat's ears.

"Ah," the frog said again and Josphat looked around, confused, because he could not tell where the sound was coming from.

"Ah," said Chura, and Josphat's heart sank. The sound was coming from the thorn bush, the same thick one into which the snake had disappeared.

This time, however, Josphat did not hesitate. He ran all the way home and all the way back, carrying a hoe, pickaxe and slasher. All Chipo saw was her man running into the yard like a madman, picking up the tools from the shed and running straight out again.

"What…" She was left standing there, her question unfinished, unanswered.

Up the hill and down the other side, Josphat was an Olympic marvel, occasionally adjusting the tools that he carried awkwardly balanced in both hands. Looking at him running without breaking stride, one could be forgiven for fearing that he might hurt himself with one of the implements.

Getting to the bush, he immediately got to work, first hacking away at the thorns with his slasher, succeeding in getting himself scratched in the process. Eventually, he tore his shirt off altogether as it was getting in the way. Beads of sweat glistened all over his body until, finally, the thorn was defeated, and he proceeded to hack the prickly twigs out of the way. With the area now cleared, Josphat backed away a little to inspect his work thus far.

He frowned in puzzlement. There was neither frog nor snake, and no water body. Just dry ground. Where was the frog that had been talking to him not long ago? And the snake? Surely it had come in here and… And then what?

Something flashed somewhere to his right and, as he turned to look, a bright light shone straight into his eyes so sharply he blinked them shut in involuntary shock. Josphat shook his head, picked up his pickaxe and averted his eyes as he approached the light, but it dimmed and almost disappeared as he got closer.

"Water," Josphat whispered in amazement and disbelief.

He gripped the pickaxe. He swung at the swampy area where the light had been shining and felt the soft clump of loose soil as the pick came down. Josphat ran back and picked up the hoe, which he now used to dig with more determination. He dug and dug and dug, the ground moisture coming up and muddying his tool. He must have gone some four metres down when he felt his legs seemingly sinking. He pulled himself up, out of the small hole he had dug so far and sat on his haunches. He needed to think. He had not hit water yet, but it was down there, he was sure of it.

"Oh, my God! You found… Did you find water? Josphat, did you… Oh my God!"

Chipo hugged her husband and started crying and

laughing with a mixture of joy, relief, excitement and every other emotion that defines love and gratitude. She had followed him, worried at what she had seen a few minutes before, fearing the love of her life had lost his mind. Josphat hugged her back with his muddied hands and soon they were both rollicking with laughter and jubilation.

"Water! Water! Water! We've got water, we've found water! Water! Water! Water! We found water!"

***

When a muddied, shirtless Josphat walked into the chief's compound with his arm around a grinning, almost equally shabby wife, the chief's aides readily stepped aside and one of them ran to the chief to announce the visitor. They knew him, of course, but there was something about his countenance and the strange aura around the couple that prevented them from asking questions if they had any. It was mysterious enough that Josphat and Chipo looked like they had been frolicking in mud. Where would they roll in mud in this dry country, where even a drop of dew attracted attention?

The buzz grew as the explanation filtered out. Excitement filled the chief's compound and soon, his headmen had assembled armed men who followed Josphat and the chief, walking side by side towards "the spot", Chipo a little way behind, knowing she should not be in the procession but caring little for it. No one thought of asking where she had left her daughter, who had been forgotten in all the hubbub.

Early in the morning two days later, the borehole rig from China Aid rolled into the village and, by the end of the day, everyone in Josphat's village had access to water.

They named it Josphat's Well. China Aid put a fence around it and built a concrete slab and protective structures around it. In time, pipes were connected so that the water would reach homes quicker, and only the chief's guards were found around Josphat's Well, watching over the place day and night.

When Simbarashe was born a year later, the entire village turned up for the christening festivities. The chief, who was guest of honour, cracked jokes at Josphat's expense, about how ragged and dirty he looked when he brazenly walked into his compound, devoid of any decorum. Even then, mystery still surrounded the source of the water and much speculation and fairy tales and myths were created which cannot be verified to this day.

Where did the water come from? It was a question asked and debated in hushed whispers, for fear of offending the spirits of the ancestors, the ones that provided the water on request.

Josphat's Well is still there in his village, preserved like a shrine. The colourful grass snake was never seen, a miraculous apparition unto its own. Villagers also said there were no frogs in the area and that Josphat's ears must have tricked him. There were many that strongly believed Josphat had been in a vision where the ancestors and Mwari made him see things no human could see, chosen because of his piety and purity of heart. For this, Josphat was feared and revered.

PAUL

PAUL was late again. I mean, we knew Paul for this annoying habit of his, never keeping time. We just could never get used to it. This time he was not only late; he was very, very late, like forty-five minutes late! By the time he arrived, we had all but given up and I, for one, secretly cursed him under my breath. I get incensed by people who cannot keep time. But I said nothing. Cosmas was around. He would tell Paul if I said anything. That was not the problem, because Cosmas seemed to live on spreading word around. His problem, which he could not help because, well, that was just him, his problem was that he would embellish – that's the word! – he would *embellish* what anyone said, so that it sounded worse than the truth. Cosmas was a snake and a Judas. So, I cursed Paul but did not let the curse escape from my mouth.

Thing is, we wanted Paul around. We needed him. Paul made the world go round. Paul made sense of everything, and he had a way of doing it that was so simple it made us all look… stupid. He knew everything. I do not know of anyone in our group who did not envy Paul, some to the point of jealousy – which was their problem, because everybody else loved Paul and would make excuses for him. Hating him, disliking him or any other negative energy towards him was just a waste of time. He paid it all no attention. He oozed confidence, lots of it, and was greatness personified. But I think some of us feared him as well, especially when he appeared triggered by views contrary to his. It was a small thing, hardly noticeable, because Paul would quickly laugh it off. Yet we all seemed to know he was a man you did not want to get on the wrong side of.

"Paul is here," Chenai said, as casually as you like. It was loud enough for everyone to perk up and, already, the atmosphere started changing. You could feel the buzz cascading up, lifting spirits in a deliberate, gradual, magnetic way that tugged at your… navel? Must have been, for a chorus of light stomach rumbles escaped, unbidden, embarrassingly so, from a few of us. As if by some witchcraft, Paul, even though not yet in sight, pulled everyone onto their feet and stopped all conversation. Only the soft, smooth jazz music from Grafton's portable unit remained unaffected and played on. That, and Chenai. She remained where she was, sitting awkwardly on a rock that looked like a sculptor had lost interest while shaping it into some kind of stool. She was wearing brown cargo pants and a beige silk top, staring expressionlessly at the meat on the fire.

Often, thinking about Chenai, I would wonder why she was in our group. She spoke very little, laughed even less, but she smiled, oh yes, she smiled, as if enjoying some personal joke. But, guffawing like the rest of us did? Never. A hot-shot economist with a private firm of white corporate consultants, Chenai came to us by some quirk of fate. I'm afraid I had something to do with it.

We were on one of our outings just like this one, at an off-the-beaten-track mini resort that Grafton and I had discovered. Grafton, Cosmas, myself, Paul, Rati and Michelle had made it a habit to look for quiet, hidden places to share our study notes while we were doing our marketing MBA course with a long-distance college. The study group had just morphed into itself and none of us could explain how we all came together because it was, I guess, spontaneous and we had developed a natural affinity to each other during classes. The group continued well after graduation, and we've been like that ever since. I was not even sure, when I first invited her, that Chenai would stay. She seemed so different, so classy, so… un-black!

On that fateful day, we ran out of drinks, and Grafton and I volunteered to dash to a shopping centre that we had passed not far back. There, I must confess, for reasons I cannot explain, I struck up a conversation with the girl in blue jeans, red shirt and dreadlocks who was picking and returning onto the shelf different bottles of wine, after studying each for lengthy periods of time. Please don't judge me. I just found her striking, but if you ask me to describe what was particularly fascinating about her, I would not be able to tell you. But someone – Cosmas, no less – told me that that is how "charm" is defined. Learning does not end.

"Spoilt for choice? Can't make up your mind?" I asked cheerfully.

She delivered a most disarming smile and said, "Wanna help?"

Cartwheels.

"What are you looking for?" I said, feigning nonchalance.

"Don't laugh, but I really don't know. I just want something to drink and drift away."

"Oooh, I hope you're not one of those that think they can drown their sorrows in drink!"

"Oh, no," she shot back. "It's the weekend and I'm bored stiff. I tried to read, I tried a movie but…"

Then, I 'shot my shot', as they say these days. "Well, if you're adventurous you could join our small bunch of do-nothings down the road and…"

My heart sank as she shook her head. "Nah, I'll pass. Have fun."

Still, I quickly regained my composure, picked a bottle of a classic merlot and extended it to her. "Try this. It's dry but not too heavy on the palate."

Her smile melted me as she curtsied playfully and said, "Wow, thank you. Are you a wine connoisseur?"

Grafton came round the corner with a case of green bottles and another of ciders. He stopped short, then grinned mischievously and came over to us.

"Ah, yah, Jonso, Jonso, Jonso! I can't leave you for two minutes."

I glared at him as he put the cases down, made as if shaking water off his right hand and thrust it at Chenai for a forced handshake, ignoring me completely. "Hi, I'm Grafton. I am with this one."

That was the only time I experienced her laugh, a short one, as she obliged the handshake. "I'm Chenai.

Your Jonso friend here is a rude nice guy. He hasn't introduced himself, but he wants me to go with him, and he got me this wine."

A thousand million emotions, chaos and confusion in my system. First of all, none of the two of us had introduced each other, and second, did I offer to buy the wine? But third and most important, had she just *pivoted* and subtly accepted my invitation?

Long story short, I bought the wine, and Chenai came with us. We convinced her to leave her car at that shopping centre, to pick it up later, on our way back. Our fears that Rati and Michelle might react badly were completely unfounded and the three ladies struck it off brilliantly. They teased me together as if they had known each other for a long time, calling me '*le* smooth operator'. Grafton joined the conspiracy – another Judas.

Why are we even talking about Chenai, when the focus should be on Paul?

He arrived loudly and in a cloud of dust, making sure he spun his wheels dramatically in a small arc, and parked neatly adjacent to my car. My heart skipped a beat when I thought he might redecorate. Then I remembered this was Paul. Show-off Paul. Perfect in everything Paul. He loved fast, loud cars, and the faster and louder, the better.

He allowed the dust to settle before opening the door. We all stood there, watching him, none of us taking so much as a step towards his car. He stepped out the way Paul steps out: emphatically, with a flourish, wide grin and arms outstretched – for the ladies, obviously.

They ran to him, except Chenai. His easy laughter and their giggles. I saw Cosmas, who had this fascinatingly strange habit of constantly pulling his right earlobe with the thumb and forefinger of his left hand, watching the spectacle coyly, no doubt conjuring up some creative script. When he finally released the ladies from his embrace, Paul came to us, and we bumped fists and shoulders in turn.

"You're here, finally," I said, returning his hard handshake and repaying stare for stare. "We've finished all the drinks and there's only fat left on the fire for you."

Paul just laughed his Paul laugh and shouted across, "Hey, Chenai!"

She waved. "Hey back. You're late again."

"But I'm here, Your Highness. Brother Paul is here."

From the get-go, Paul called Chenai 'Your Highness'. His reason? "She's up there, where the subjects know better than to disturb her peace. She's confident and speaks little. Only kings and queens do that."

Enough time wasted. Paul helped himself to a bottle of beer and we got into the discussion about our impending project. Paul and Chenai, not surprisingly, astonished us with their insights, and the whole thing started to make sense.

"See?" Paul said triumphantly. "She's not Her Highness for nothing!"

Chenai curtsied and we all laughed. Curtsying was another of her trademarks.

Paul talking about someone else's confidence always intrigued me. He was himself the epitome of it. Physically, he was not the towering picture that you would expect for such an imposing character. He was of average height but athletic looking enough. He only looked tall because he stood tall, accentuating it with high boots most of the time. Not too dark in complexion, but not too light either. Not too handsome but not too much on the other side either. Not too rich but not too much in want either. In short, like the rest of us, Paul was just a regular Joe, with a modest job as an artisan with a well-known foundry in the city's industrial sites. Why the MBA? Just for kicks, he said. Just for kicks? Who does that? Every other one of us did it for career development ambitions.

But there was something about Paul. Charming Paul. Happy-go-lucky, never-a-dull-moment Paul. Confident, in-your-face Paul. Creative Paul. Funny, comedic Paul. Effervescent and ebullient Paul.

Tardy Paul. Yet reassuring, spirit-lifting Paul. There was something about Paul.

It was Chenai who finally unravelled it for us. All these years that we had known Paul, and it took a *mafikizolo*, a yesterday-lass who spoke little, laughed less and was almost a misfit, only a handful of outings to figure him out.

I'll tell you how Chenai did it in a minute. Before I do that, I want to let you know that Paul's stature grew even more in our eyes after Chenai opened a box she was not supposed to open. We respected him more, exalted him even, not quite to godly stature on account of some of his annoying habits and discomfiting traits. Such as his tardiness. Such as his *overwhelming-ness*. His jokes could be dry too, on occasion. For many weeks after, I would catch each of us stealing furtive glances at Paul, trying to figure him out further, perhaps? I wasn't immune to that myself, and one day I was jolted by Chenai glaring at me reprimand-fashion when she caught me staring at Paul. I must have done so for a long time because her headshake was vigorous, and her lips were set heavily against each other. I imagined the teeth being gritted in there and any captured air having to escape through the chiselled cavities of her small nose.

Like the rest of my friends, I had questions about Paul after Chenai carved him open. Yet all the questions led to one simple answer: Paul was a strong character. Full stop. We are where we are today because of Paul. And we were waiting for him on this day to finalise our project concept knowing how valuable his thoughts were. It happened to be his birthday, too. By the time he arrived, though, our plan to serenade him with the birthday song had evaporated and we only gaped at him, embraced him in welcome and then got straight down to business. Michelle only reminded us some twenty minutes later that we ought also to be celebrating his birthday.

I am backing and forth-ing too much, aren't I? You're curious about Chenai's tactlessness in the Great Reveal of Paul the Enigma, right? Here's how it happened.

It was about two months or so after Chenai had allowed herself to join our small group, being bored and courtesy of curiosity and the expensive wine that I was compelled to buy, as well as gentle persuasion from Grafton and me. After other nothing-to-write-home-about venues, we had decided we would go back to that same secret mini resort that we had discovered because it had a great ambience: little dam features corralled into natural rock, small dams teeming with colourful aquatic life, furtively sited accommodations and spacious braai areas, even a glittering swimming pool and a large football-pitch size open space featuring a well-manicured lawn. The whole place was a soothing profusion of cool, green and shady trees and shrubbery, and the happy sounds of free birds and insects made for absolute mental therapy. Grafton's smooth jazz was perfectly suited to the natural, pollution-free world that was Our Secret Place.

It was a day of lazy fun, and we had agreed not to spend too much time on the project for a change. We wanted to have a relaxed afternoon with our drinks and our inevitable roast beef, chicken and sausages with raw salads. Grafton's non-intrusive Afro-jazz music. Cracking jokes, funny and un-funny, it didn't matter. All we wanted was to pass the time idly with people we were cosy with. That's all we wanted. Chenai spoilt it all for us. But she also did us a hell of a lot of good.

"Paul?" Chenai said, choosing with perfect timing one of those sudden silent moments that happen in every group. The Unfinished Sculpture Stone Stool that nature had thrown here had become her uncontested, unspoken throne and she had found a way of depositing her bum neatly and comfortably on it. That day, she even had the luxury of removing her shoes and crossing her legs in an alluring 4 that only served to tease our perverted brains, her cargo pants patriotically following the contours of the lower part of her body, and the top buttons of her matching silk shirt naughtily open just enough for us to see a little chest skin and lifted breast.

We had just had a good laugh at a joke that I no longer have any recollection of. I just remember we still had our smiles plastered on our faces, like a frozen photographic moment. Those smiles vanished slowly, like a movie fading to black.

"What's up, Highness?" Paul said cheerfully.

She stared at him for a while, as if mentally arranging her words but, in truth, she was waiting for Paul to look directly at her. He did and, perhaps sensing something, frowned a little.

"Did someone hurt you?" Chenai said eventually, in a smooth and flat, even tone.

"Whaat?" Paul's response was like a shocked whisper. His whole countenance transmogrified before our very eyes. He shot daggers at Chenai and opened his mouth again. But he didn't speak. He was starting to breathe heavily, his chest heaving perceptibly.

We all were stunned into silence and all we could do was look from one to the other, puzzled by what we could not understand.

Chenai neither flinched nor showed any emotion under Paul's glare. She merely inclined her head and kept staring at him. Then she asked, "When you were little, did someone hurt you?"

Paul pressed his lips together tightly. His chest heaved. Up, down, up, down. We had never seen him like this. Unbidden, Grafton switched off the happy song that was starting to play after the silence. Rati, who was standing next to me, came closer and cuddled up and I instinctively put my arm around her. She was breathing too, in panicked, fast, rhythmic beats. A little way off, Michelle got off the bonnet of the car where she had been sitting, unworried that her short skirt was showing off too much light skin. She walked over to where we were and leaned against the driver's door, her chest arching forward like a supermodel. She was chewing on a piece of grass, holding aloft her bottle of half-finished cider. Cosmas once complained that these girls took us too much for granted. I said it was a good sign that they were comfortable around us. Cosmas himself, for once, stopped rubbing his earlobe.

A pin dropped. We all heard it.

"Paul?" Chenai prompted again, showing neither fear nor sign of relenting.

Still, Paul stared at her and said nothing. His eyes were now a fiery red and were beginning to show some wetness in them. Looking back, I realised Paul was fighting an inner emotion, trying to control himself, deciding whether to attack Chenai or some other reaction. His breathing became slower gradually, more controlled, like one who had been taught to count to ten in such situations.

Just when the tension seemed too much to bear for the rest of us who had no idea what was going on, Chenai got up and, still barefooted, walked slowly over to Paul. Then a strange thing happened; she offered him both her hands, palms outwards, like some priestess. Paul looked at those hands for a while, seemed to hesitate and then slowly took them.

"Look at me, Paul," Chenai said, speaking slowly in a low but clear, commanding voice and looking directly into his eyes. We might as well not have been there, the way she completely ignored us and everything around us. Paul was her undivided focal point. "Look at me," she said softly. "It's ok. We are all your friends here. Come, it's ok. Come."

And she slowly pulled him to her. He came into her arms without protest, like a child, as if lured by some magic, as if grateful for the intrusion into his life.

"It's ok," she repeated in a gentle whisper, as she embraced and hugged the man, whose chin could rest on the crown of her head. He hugged her back and she started rubbing his back, slowly, then…

Big, confident Paul wept. He shook heavily and started sobbing loudly, openly. Chenai held him tighter, with more determination, and rocked him more, as if consoling a baby. She kept whispering in his ear, reassurances that we only occasionally picked up. Us, that were now even more puzzled but also scared by the spectacle before us. Michelle turned away and gripped the car, Grafton and Cosmas held each other's hands tightly and I felt Rati's tears on my chest. We had all become a real spectacle, if anyone had been looking. It was as if someone had just broken news of the death of a loved one.

I'm not sure how long this continued. All I can tell you is that, if nothing else had solidified and cemented our friendship and solidarity, this single incident did. We went from anger and bitterness with Chenai to revering her, for she made Paul into a better version of himself. She confessed later that she had worked on a hunch, because of a personal experience with a cousin who, unfortunately, took his own life when he felt too overwhelmed. She said her cousin also displayed faux confidence, was a motivational speaker who liked to laugh and joke a lot but had the same "dead eyes" that she saw in Paul during the times when he seemed lost in thought.

Paul had dead eyes? We had not noticed any of that. For me, it made Chenai herself an interesting character indeed, and I resolved to spend more time learning *her*!

She was right. Someone did hurt Paul, when he was little.

After all the drama and tension, Paul eventually extricated himself from Chenai and she released him gently.

He smiled wanly at each of us in turn. His whole shirtfront was wet with tears, which he had generously poured onto Chenai's shirt as well, whose eyes were red and wet too.

Paul tried to speak and only managed a squeak. He cleared his throat and smiled again in embarrassment. "Sorry, guys."

We shrugged and shook our heads. We all laughed an uneasy laugh when Grafton violently shook his hand out of Cosmas's, as if only then realising they were still holding hands.

Paul said in a low, uncharacteristic, halting voice, "Um, guys, I have something to tell you."

When he said this, he was looking at Chenai, who pursed her lips and nodded encouragingly. Rati came off my chest, and we all found somewhere to sit: large enough rocks for Grafton and I, back seats of cars in the case of Michelle, Rati and Cosmas, and for Chenai, her little throne.

Paul remained standing and now looked like an Influence, about to address his minions, if you observed from afar.

He cleared his throat, looked skyward then at the ground, and finally, directly at us. He sighed a heavy sigh.

"Chenai is right," he said at last. "When I was little, I was abused several times by relatives…"

We sat up collectively, even Chenai, but she nodded in understanding. Paul pursed his lips again and held up his hand, as if to curtail any reaction from us. What he told us was heart-rending, to say the least and, as much as we're told through news media that these things happen, they shouldn't. We felt real anger, an aggravated rage that I had never thought I could experience, perhaps because it was this close to home.

Paul told us that his clear recollections only went as far back as when he was six or seven years old. His parents had died in a car crash when he was only three. He was their only child and survived the crash because he was asleep in his cot in the back seat. They had only been married five years. His mother's sister took him, but tragedy followed tragedy when this aunt, already diagnosed with colon cancer when she took him in, died in her sleep when he was almost five years old. He was told his paternal grandparents had also died and his maternal ones had divorced and were living new lives with new families, so he remained in the care of his uncle.

Paul said he was sure the abuse started around then. His uncle remarried less than a year later, and Paul's life turned upside down. He said he remembered going to Aunty Miranda, the maid, to complain that he was feeling funny between his bums. She examined him and then started to rub where the pain was, then proceeded to rub his little pee-pee. He said it felt good and, each time uncle did something to him between his bums, he would go to Aunty Miranda. This went on for a long time until he went to school and his class teacher asked him why he "walked funny". He had no idea what she meant, and the teacher took him to the headmaster and, before he could understand what was going on, a doctor and nurse from the local clinic came, accompanied by some police details.

A week later, his uncle, his new aunt and Aunty Miranda were picked up by the police on charges of child abuse and conspiracy to abuse. Paul said he was then taken into a children's home, where he continued with school until he finished his primary education. When he finished, he found himself in another home, this time for senior boys graduating into their teenage years and secondary school. Here, Paul paused, bit his lips, looked skyward again and breathed another huge sigh.

"The abuse started again," he said. He shook his head vigorously, as if to erase the memory.

It was some of the much older boys, the principal and one of the matrons. Paul said he hatched a plan to escape with two classmates who had had similar experiences. They shared that they felt trapped and had to get away but feared they might not be able to survive out there, to support themselves. They resolved to risk it and leave anyway. They were going to school at a government college not far from the home and left as normal one morning. On the way to school, they broke away, ditched their school uniforms for some clothes they had smuggled out of the home and, with money stolen from the matron's purse when she left it on her desk, hiked to Bindura, a small town where they joined other boys and girls on the streets.

"I was now officially a street kid," Paul said.

It was to become the boy's new normal. Paul found

himself able to reinvent himself quickly and forget about the low self-esteem that the abuse had caused in him. It was necessary to come out of the shell if he was to survive. He learned to assert himself and, in time, became leader of a motley crew of eight or nine pickpockets, boys and girls. They had strict rules: no stealing from old men and women, no stealing from primary school children, no stealing from beggars or other vagabonds. They bought food and clothes with the money they stole, which they shared equally. Soon, however, their luck ran out. Paul thought one of his crew members snitched or it was a well-worked trap by someone who had been studying their ways. Whichever it was, quite a number of the crew members were picked up by the police over the course of three days. Paul himself and another girl managed to evade them and fled back to Harare. He was sure no one would recognise him as he was now a teenager and spotted a small goatee.

Some five years had passed since his escape from the boys' home. One day, the girl with whom he had fled came to announce that there was an old woman asking about him who was camping at the entrance to the church where, once a week, the urchins and other homeless people queued for soup rations and, sometimes, second-hand clothes. As much as possible, Paul avoided that church and depended on the girl to bring him things. Always hiding under a cap pulled low, she would go disguised as a boy with a stammer and a limp in his left leg. Paul called her Samantha, but we suspect it wasn't her real name. He had given himself a new name from the time of the first escape and was known throughout the "street years" as Spencer.

Unknown to him, the arrest of the notorious Pickpocket Kids of Bindura had made headlines across local news channels. He was a wanted man, and pictures of "Spencer" and "Samantha" were plastered on the front or prominent pages of the most circulated papers and on national television. In a subsequent investigative story, one newspaper broke the news that "Spencer" was one of three boys that had escaped from a boys' home after stealing money and various items, and that his name was, in fact, Paul Gabvu. Aside from suggesting they suspected Paul and "Samantha" had escaped to Harare, the two other boys from the children's home would not be drawn into saying anything else. Despite spirited protestations about being taken back to the home, the boys were forced back there on threats of being locked up for at least five years each. No one wanted to hear their story. A week later, they were found dead in their shared dormitory, having apparently conspired to jointly swallow rat poison.

Paul shook his head. "Where had they got it? They killed my friends. They were not suicidal. *They* killed them, rather than face the shame and embarrassment of their story coming out. I know they killed them."

The sun was setting. We only noticed it when Paul looked up at the sky and appeared to rush past the finer details of his story. He said "Samantha" tried to persuade him to see the old lady because she kept asking about him, but no one could help. Paul said he had no relatives that he knew about. When she couldn't break through his stubbornness, Samantha took matters into her own hands and, one soup day, came to their hideout with the old woman in tow.

"Samantha and that old woman saved my life, and made me believe again," Paul said, fighting back tears.

At 82 years of age, the old woman turned out to be Paul's paternal grandmother. What of the news that both his father's parents had died? She appeared surprised at this at first and was silent for some time. Then she nodded as if at some revelation, forced a smile and said it didn't matter anymore now. She confirmed that many of his father's family had, indeed, died, and when she found out that the in-laws who were supposed to be looking after her grandson were serving jail terms for abusing him, she intensified her search. She told Paul how she had looked for him for the last fourteen years. By the time she got to the boys' home, Paul had already escaped. But she told him she knew he was out there somewhere and waited and waited, praying fervently that God delivered him to her. And now, wasn't God great?

Ambuya took Paul and Samantha to her rural home where everyone helped her celebrate the return of the grandson she had spent almost two decades searching for. The village headman and community leaders agreed to hide Paul from the police and the two rehabilitated teenagers attended formal school as twins. Paul was active in club sports and was popular in the Debate Team, where he also learned about leadership. Ironically, his experience as a gang leader helped him gain in confidence. He said when he left school, he opted to take up apprenticeship training in foundry and casting. He found employment at the company where he had done his practical internship, and the owner told him he needed him to up his skills and "follow the value chain".

Paul smiled. "I didn't join the MBA class for kicks.

The boss is paying for it. He also gave me the loan to buy that car." He continued, "If you noticed, I kept pretty much to myself at first. But that man," he pointed at Cosmas, "does not know how to mind his own business and, truth be told, I only joined your study group to stop him pestering me."

We gaped at Cosmas, the Gossip. He rewarded us with a little wave and a smile and resumed feeling his earlobe. Wonders never cease, I thought.

"Thanks to him, I found my real family." Paul wasn't finished. "You guys just don't know what you've done. Chenai saw through me, and she is right. This arrogant, confident act is just for show. I am an actor. This is not the real me. I was broken and hopeless and knew no support from anyone, until my granny came. For their selfish reasons, they made me believe that she had died along with all my father's relatives, but they lied. She's old and frail now, and I go to see her whenever I can, on those weekends when you don't see me. Since the day I found you, my life now makes sense and one day, one day I'll tell my story for all the abused kids out there."

There was silence for quite a while as we all grappled with what we had just heard.

"What about Samantha?" I finally asked the question on everyone's mind.

"Oh. We – the village, my grandmother and I – helped her across the border. She's happy now, she has a good job and family, a whole new life. She's got a new identity and I'm happy for her. She's a real sister, the one and only true sister I ever had. She deserves her peace. But I also have new sisters now."

Our three girls smiled sad smiles, and Michelle wiped

off a tear with the back of a forefinger. We knew not to prod further. Silence reigned again for a while.

Paul turned to Chenai and started to say, good-naturedly, "Your Highness," but then his voice broke, and he was a jumble of emotion one more time. He sobbed openly. Chenai jumped up as we all rushed to him in one accord, to smother him in a group embrace, sharing each other's tears and perhaps, silently, each other's personal stories as well. Everyone has their own, but none more so than the rollercoaster Paul had just taken us through.

WHILE THE HOUSE BURNED

THE fly is not the most pleasant of insects. Neither is the cockroach.

Masimba contemplated both with genuine, equal disgust as he fought to absorb the sting of his wife's verbal assault.

The cockroach settled on a drop of drying soup. Its mate, the fly, did a few acrobatics above him and his soup before making a gentle landing a short distance away, rubbing its hands in excited anticipation. The cockroach ignored the antics, its full concentration fixed on the meal it was having. It did not seem to Masimba as if anything was happening to the little driblet of soup, but he knew if he looked away long enough, there would be nothing there when he looked back. In their disgusting way, they were funny creatures, cockroaches, and Masimba wondered how anything could thrive on filth.

Flies were worse, he thought, turning his attention to the cockroach's mate. As if aware that it had an audience, it showed off to him by taking off without taxiing and performed a few acrobatics at high speed before it landed again, so close to the cockroach that the latter seemed to jump in fright. The fly settled on top of the soup. If it had a flag, Masimba had no doubt it would have waved it left and right triumphantly and pitched it to announce its conquest for the whole world to see.

As his wife's verbiage grew louder the more he appeared not to be listening. Masimba made even more concerted efforts to ignore her, to shut her voice out. Once started, there was no stopping Gladys, who could speak so fast it was a wonder she never tripped over her own words. To make matters worse, she had one of those high-pitched voices whose inflections define vocal discord. Masimba found it sharp, strident and irritating to the extreme. He could not recall why he had not noticed it when they were dating and could only remember a rather reserved, smiling, coy girl who spoke very little. Now, he thought, she squawked rather than spoke, and her voice always struck in him images of a hen loudly protecting its eggs or young against a slithering reptile. When Gladys started, one could not get a word in, and his response was to let her get on with it until she got tired. This unfortunately only served to irritate her more and make her worse.

"Why don't you speak?" she squawked now. "How can you stay quiet? Are you trying to make me look stupid? Are you trying to tell me that I'm talking nonsense? Because I know you! That's what your silence means. You think what I am saying is not worth listening to! You've always thought I'm unintelligent and you have a very low opinion of me! You think you made a mistake marrying me! If that is not the case then answer me, say something! Eh. You see! You don't want to say anything because you do not speak to stupid people!"

And so it went. It was always like this these days. Ever since the children had gone away to boarding school, Gladys had become irritable. Masimba raised his head as he suddenly realised that she *had* always shouted. Her venom, however, had always been directed at the kids, either the boy or the girl, whoever was close by. Listening to her, you would think none of them ever got anything right, and Gladys often accused them of conspiring against her, especially when she found them talking in low tones. Now that they were safely out of the way of her sharp tongue, Gladys directed her vitriol at the next best object, her husband.

The cockroach recovered and retrieved his meal from his mate. The fly gave up, flew high briefly, then taxied down dramatically in a swooping motion, to settle on the edge of the plate of uneaten food in front of Masimba. He watched it in fascination. It locomoted in short, sharp jerks into the food, mistimed its footing and landed in the gravy, where it promptly got stuck. Masimba felt sick and pushed the plate away.

"So! Now you don't want to eat your food?" Gladys shrieked. "You waste so much food. Or you eat somewhere else? If you don't want to eat here, why don't you just say so!"

Then she saw the fly in the soup.

"Aha, you see!" she cried, almost triumphantly. "You

see! And I know you don't like flies. So, who do you think is going to eat that?" She shook her head. "What a waste."

She picked up the plate and headed for the kitchen sink, muttering something about feeding the dogs with all the left-over food. Seeing the golden opportunity for escape, Masimba stood up and strode rapidly out of the kitchen to get the car keys. He resolved that he was not going to sit around in a house in which he was the target of such verbal diarrhoea. A game of pool with the boys, maybe some darts and a bottle or two of beer wouldn't be amiss and might help cool the nerves a bit. Such nagging was the excuse his mates also used in order to get away from home… and who could blame them? He collected his keys in the bedroom and turned for the door.

Gladys was blocking it.

"Aaand where does it think it is going?" she inquired in dangerous, drawling tones, upper lip lifted with the aid of the left part of the nose, a trait Masimba found annoying. "Let me tell you, you are not going anywhere!"

She paused long enough to appraise him from head to toe, then pronounced, "Ahem, man with a big tummy! It is not going anywhere. We, the stupid Gladyses of this world, are the ones left behind to battle with the welfare of some, some, some stupid selfish men who do not even appreciate the amount of sacrifices we make for them. We cook, you don't eat. We clean the house, you don't notice. We do the washing up of your clothes and the blankets you sleep and fart in, and there's not even a small thank you! Do you know the amount of trouble I go to for you, Big Tummy? Do you? You're just concentrating on making that tummy bigger."

Masimba was now getting impatient and agitated and finally spoke up. "Gladys, don't be silly. Get out of the w—"

"Silly? Silly? Who is being silly? That's exactly what I am saying! This, this, this name calling, this despising, this looking-down-on… stupid, silly! Me? Me, silly? Huh?"

"Get out of the way, Gladys. I want to go to the pub."

"Oh ho! Pub. That's all you ever think about. In fact, I have my doubts…"

She didn't finish the sentence deliberately, and Masimba rolled his eyes and thought, here we go again. She's manufacturing another floozy for me, and I now really wish I had one. He threw himself onto the bed in resignation and then, almost as suddenly, sat bolt upright and sniffed the air loudly.

"I think you're burning something," he told Gladys.

"*Ngazvitsve*, let it burn!" came the unpleasant rejoinder. "There is no one to eat it anyway. I know your tricks, my friend."

As she launched into another lengthy tirade of how he failed to appreciate her cooking, Masimba lay back on the bed, closed his eyes and absorbed the verbiage. At some point he drifted off to sleep and dreamt of being chased by the ogre in one of his grandmother's old tales, told as they sat around a fire in pleasant, old, moonlit, rural Mhondoro, popping and eating salted dried maize toasted in an oval makeshift metal pan. They later found out that it was the lid of a steel bin that had long since been battered to death by months and years of being an amateur drummers' instrument of choice at new year celebrations.

The ogre wore layers and layers of skirts as old, worn and tattered as she was. She never wore a doek or headdress of any kind, and her hair was twisted in long dirty locks that stretched down to the waist. Her very black hands were calloused, characterised by the longest fingernails he had ever seen. She always wore an ugly, frightening grin, displaying pink-brown toothless gums. Probably just as well because if she had teeth, Masimba reckoned they would be the dirtiest yellow. She walked slowly, with a stoop, aided by a long, slender walking stick that was shaped like a snake. In grandmother's story, this stick came alive at night and became the old hag's companion with whom she wreaked havoc on unsuspecting, naughty children who disobeyed their parents.

The old hag beckoned with one long fingernail for Little Masimba to come to her. Masimba took one look at her and said never, not in a thousand years. He sought assistance from his feet and they complied. He ran-flew from the ogre, as fast as his tiny legs could carry him. Twice he fell as he ran, but he kept pulling himself up and running as he heard the hag's shrill voice calling out his name. Each time, she sounded closer, no matter how fast he ran and Masimba felt himself tiring, running out of breath.

"Wake up, stupid! Masimba, wake up!" Gladys was shaking her husband violently and, if he didn't know better, he would say she was in a state of panic, so wide-eyed was she. He rubbed his eyes and shook his head.

She *was* in a state of panic. "The house is burning,

Masimba!" she screamed, at almost the same time he caught the strong smell of smoke.

Masimba rushed past her to the kitchen, but the smoke was overpowering, and the flames were already too big and threw him back. Tongues of flame lashed at him. He rushed back to the bedroom, picked up Gladys as if she were a doll and crash-jumped through the bedroom window into the safety of the backyard, where helping hands relieved him of his load and dragged his tired body to safety. They wrapped him in a blanket, for the shock.

The well-trained men from the fire brigade did a good job of it and took just over an hour to douse the flames completely. In her own borrowed blanket, a short distance away, Gladys watched in stunned, silent bemusement. She turned and stared long and hard at her husband. Was that a new softness in her eyes? She walked over to him and sat beside him. Slowly, as if fearing he might break, she put an arm gently around him and started rocking the both of them to the accompaniment of quiet sobs… her own.

PUT TO GOOD USE

A Short Film

FADE IN
EXT. RURAL SETTING -- DAY.

We are flying slowly over village huts scattered over a grassy, treed expanse, featuring rural pathways, small rivers and streams. We hear the natural sounds of birds, cocks crowing, dogs barking, the occasional cow mooing, as we fly down into the village and one particular homestead floats up to meet us.

CUT TO
EXT. SIMPLE RURAL HOMESTEAD, GRANARY
ON STILTS, TWO OTHER HUTS METRES APART.

Panning slowly from one end to another, we see an empty cattle pen. There are a few chickens running around chasing each other, lying down or scraping the ground. A medium-size mongrel dog lies under a mango tree, seemingly asleep.

CUT TO C/UP ROUND HUT OFF CENTRE OF YARD.
DISSOLVE TO. INT. OF HUT

Elfanos Mwandipirei, a slight man of average stature, is walking around. Furniture is sparse, showing shelves and cupboards with a sparse assortment of utensils. A table is at one end, covered with a multicoloured cloth of African print design. On one shelf we see a small shining portable radio, showing signs of age but also tender care. Elfanos advances towards shelf and radio. He pulls it gently off the shelf, walks with it to the table, all the while fiddling with antenna and controls, seeking a station. He sets it down gently on the table and starts to walk to a small stool as it crackles to life and music wafts from it, then starts to fade slowly.

RADIO VOICE: That was the sound of King Sounds and the Israelites, with Book of Rules, a song that was popular in this country in the early years of our independence, bringing to an end this session of Dzakamboita Mukurumbira, the songs that we used to sing along and dance to many years ago. Join us again next week, same day, same time, same channel, if you like going back in time.

Radio signature tune music up and under.

RADIO VOICE: You are tuned in to the Zimbabwe Broadcasting Corporation, broadcasting on FM and on shortwave throughout the country. It is now two o'clock and it is time for the news…

Elfanos walks back to table, face looking expectant and pulls one of four chairs around the table, sits and pulls front of radio towards himself. He pulls antenna once more, for good measure and sits back to listen.

Suddenly, he perks up and sits bolt upright. He picks up the radio and puts it to his ear.

NEWS READER: …was speaking in Parliament yesterday. Let's hear him speak…

PARLIAMENTARIAN: The programme will be rolled out in the next few weeks once all logistics are finalised. As Government, we are saying we want to uplift the standards of our people in the rural areas by empowering them. So, we shall give them money to invest in projects, thereby removing the need for handouts. Government does not want a nation of beggars…

Elfanos has an expression of bemusement on his face. The Newsreader is hardly audible now as we close up on Elfanos's grinning face. He is mumbling to himself and throwing downward punches into his lap.

CUT TO:
EXT. DISTRICT COUNCIL OFFICES. SAME DAY, LATE AFTERNOON
Camera walks us into the fenced yard, past the old and tired buildings with their peeling fading walls, cracked windows and drooping rusted gutters. We see Elfanos sitting on a concrete bench under a tree shade

with his friend, Trust Zvourere, a clerk at the district administrator's office. Trust is dressed in a checked brown suit, purple shirt and very large yellow tie around the shirt's double collar. The tie is hanging from just below the collar bone, and the shirt's top button is undone. He completes the fashion statement with dusty brown shoes and bright yellow socks, which are visible both because Trust is sitting, and the trouser length is too short.

Elfanos is still smiling broadly.

Trust has his chest thrust forward, speaking in a low, confident tone.

TRUST: Yah, that is how it is, *bhururu*. Us, we already sent our application as soon as the circular came from Cendro Govamend. In the meeting, the DA said we are waiting for the forms and the money. It should come very soon.

ELFANOS: I like Govamend. Govamend makes me happy.

Trust leans forward and beckons his friend to do likewise, to share a secret sotto voce.

TRUST: Many people are putting their names on the waiting list. I have put yours there already. You lost your wife, you lost your brother, you have his kids to look after, so you must benefit. You didn't benefit in the goat scheme last time. But this time, this time I will make sure, for you, my friend. You will benefit. You are my good friend, and we must look out for each other.

ZOOM OUT

The two friends continue talking animatedly, laughing and joking at stories we cannot hear. From a distance, we see them stand up and start walking towards the open gate.

BLACKOUT
ON SCREEN: "THREE MONTHS LATER"

EXT. ELFANOS'S COMPOUND – DAY

We see Elfanos in tattered dirty overalls, making holes in a field in straight rows the way he and other villagers were taught by the agronomist. Sometimes we see him at one end of the field. Sometimes we see him wiping sweat off his brow with the back of his hand. As we follow him now carefully dropping two, sometimes three, maize seeds into the holes, we follow his faraway gaze and fade to a monochromatic flashback.

First, we see a man of strong physique and features, wearing neat blue overalls and white gumboots. He is standing akimbo, nodding his head sombrely at several workers milking black-and-white cows. They are dressed like the man but also wear white rubber gloves and their heads are covered by hairnets.

We look back at Elfanos, and find he is looking somewhere else, sadness in his eyes, and we follow.

CUT TO.
FLASHBACK - B/W

EXT. FUNERAL GATHERING -- DAY

Men sitting in groups, women busying themselves, smoke from several fires in the air. A priest (we identify him by his grey suit, shirt and white collar) is talking pointedly to Elfanos, who has his arms around two young children. They are the orphans of his brother, who has just been buried. Elfanos bends down to talk to them before they run off.

Now we see a young man, early 20s, well-dressed in the manner of urbanites, arguing with Elfanos.

KARIKOGA: It's just that you don't know. Things are tough, baba!

ELFANOS: You're always saying that. When did you last send money, or groceries? When did you last visit? If it wasn't for your uncle's funeral... as it is we won't see you again. How do you expect me to look after your uncle's children on my own?

KARIKOGA: I will try to send school fees; you won't be alone.

He pauses and bites his lips, resumes his bitter tone.

KARIKOGA (Cont'd): But nothing is working, baba, I keep telling you! These people are taking us backwards. They only think of their stomachs and their families. This Government has failed. Right now there is no fuel in the country, we are buying from tuckshops because the shops are empty, many young people have no jobs, the hospitals have no medi...

ELFANOS: There you go again with your lies! I am looked after by Govamend here, because you won't. How come Shungu Store has everything? You said there is no paraffin but it's there at Shungu.

Elfanos is getting angrier, and his voice is rising.

ELFANOS (Cont'd): Garikai's children come home in their cars every weekend but you, my son, all you know is complaining Govamend this, Govamend that. Was it not Govamend money that sent you to school? *Iweka*!

KARIKOGA: This is why I don't like talking to you. You were brainwashed and will never see that we need new leaders who are able…

DISSOLVE TO PRESENT DAY
EXT. FIELD -- DAY
Elfanos is shaking his head and hoeing frantically in another part of the field. Suddenly he stops and looks towards the road, where we see Trust cycling frantically towards him. He is leaning forward, half bent off the bicycle seat and his jacket is flying behind him. Dust trails him as he speeds closer into view.

He is shouting excitedly as he jumps acrobatically off the still-moving bicycle, which crashes in a heap in the yard and is promptly forgotten.

TRUST: It's here! It's here!

Both start laughing together.

TRUST (Cont'd): Bhururu! Bhururu! The money for projects has come! MP is coming this weekend and will distribute. There is a rally at the school. You are going to benefit, my friend, just like I told you!

CUT TO:
ELEVEN MONTHS LATER...
WIDE VIEW, EXT. ELFANOS'S HOUSE -- DAY
We are now seeing a transformed homestead with two farm-brick outbuildings with asbestos roofing, atop one of which sit two medium-size solar panels. In the distance and slightly off to the right, a cow milking shed with three black-and-white cows inside where the old pen used to be.

ZOOM IN.
Reveal Elfanos on stool, whistling and milking one cow.

DISSOLVE TO. ENTRANCE TO THE ELFANOS HOMESTEAD.
A white four-by-four vehicle is approaching, heavy dust mushrooming in its wake. Two officious-looking young men similarly dressed in dark suits and white shirts with red ties get out and stride purposefully towards the milking shed and Elfanos. From a distance, we espy animated discussion, Elfanos now up and gesticulating wildly.

ZOOM IN. C/UP ON ELFANOS.

ELFANOS: I tell you I didn't waste any of it! I put it to good use, just like the MP said we should. I put it to good use!

GOVERNMENT OFFICIAL 1: Sekuru, we need a record of what you did so that we can report back to head office.

GOVERNMENT OFFICIAL 2: (appearing agitated, less patient) You can't just say you put it to good use. What exactly did you do and where are the records? We need to know that!

ELFANOS: Why?

GO2: Because you haven't paid a cent back! Because it wasn't your money in the first place!

ELFANOS: (turning to GO1) *Ari kuti chiiko uyu* – what's this one saying? Is he crazy? I was given this money by Govamend. A lot of us were given this money. How can you stand there and say it is not my money? Whose son are you? The MP came here…

GO1: Sekuru, Sekuru, Sekuru! We did not come here to accuse you of anything, but Government just wishes to know.

ELFANOS: Govamend, Govamend, it is Govamend himself… *iwe!* If you came here to borrow my bicycle, it is not my business to tell you where to go with that bicycle or, or, to know what you're…

GO1: As long as I bring it back?

ELFANOS: What? What? *Eheka!* Well, yes, of course but what I am sa…

GO2: (triumphantly, cottoning on) It's the same thing, old man! Now Government wants to know what you have done with the money it lent you because you were supposed to start paying back last month! It was a loan!

ELFANOS: (Looks stunned. Pleading look at GO1) *Ndizvo, nhai muzukuru?* Is that right? In the radio…

GO1: I'm afraid so, Sekuru. So, what did you use it for? This dairy project?

ELFANOS: (dumping himself heavily on stool and putting head between hands) But I have no money, my sons! I have no money. I used it all.

Suddenly looks up and smiles brightly

ELFANOS *(Cont'd)*: But I put it to good use. The MP said we must put it to good use. I put it to good use! If he comes, he will see!

GO2: What did you do?

ELFANOS: I sent my children to school. I bought solar for this house, which I renovated with some of the money. I dug a new well. I fenced my yard and I bought two dairy cattle. Now I have three. I put it to good use, you see, my sons, I put it to good use!

GO1 looks at GO2, who shrugs his shoulders and thrusts both hands deep into his pockets. Suddenly he starts to laugh. GO1 joins him and though puzzled by this turn of events, Elfanos joins the laughter.

FADE TO BLACK…

WE WILL TAKE IT FROM HERE, THANKS

"HOW does anyone dump a kid as beautiful as this?" Solomon Manyika lamented. He pulled the light cloth covering the little girl's face further down, to take a better look, all the while shaking his head.

"The only thing I was relieved about," his wife, Maria, responded, "was that at least the mother, or whoever it was, didn't kill it."

The baby made a choked sound as if to cry and Maria shushed and rocked her in her arms. A second later however, the baby was in full cry, sending the couple into a state of panicked anxiety.

"Aw, she's messed herself!" Maria said and rushed out of the room.

When she came back a good half hour later, the baby

was glowing clean, in fresh wraps and smelt of talcum powder. With no better things to do and uninterested in the world around her, she was clutching and sucking for dear life, the tit of a feeding bottle.

Demetria and Zviko burst into the room. A stream of questions issued from them as they crowded around their mother.

"She's so cute!" Zviko said after they were told who it was. "Can I hold her?"

"Aw, look!" said Demetria. "Her eyes are smiling."

As indeed they seemed to be.

Maria had to repeat the story to all her children each time one walked in. She was a nurse aide at the local clinic. Earlier that day, after she had finished work, she had heard the muffled cries of a baby just by the bougainvillea bush outside the clinic gate. She went to investigate and found this baby, neatly wrapped and carefully placed where a passer-by could easily see it. Maria wondered if no one else had passed by. She picked the baby up and took her back to the matron, who told Maria she needed to take the baby to the police, so that the parent or parents could be traced. She and the other staff had seemed reluctant to even touch the baby, so Maria had brought it home. They had agreed with Solomon to visit the police station the next day. From the time his wife arrived with the baby, Solomon kept shaking his head and sighing.

Solomon Domingo Manhica wasn't originally from here. He had crossed the border from Mozambique a long time back, in search of a better life and because, he said, Matsanga had invaded his small town, killing, maiming and raping ruthlessly. Once here, it was only a matter of time before he changed the spelling of his last name to suit the language of the area, a province coincidentally also named Manyikaland, land of the Manyika people. His town was almost deserted when Solomon fled with the others, some finding their way into refugee camps and others, like him, opting to try their luck in the border town, Mutare. Solomon said he had no known relatives left and gradually assimilated into the community.

It wasn't too difficult to fit in. He spoke the language, since people on either side of the border could easily cross over and interact with each other. He also had a handy skill that made him useful; he made and repaired furniture, and once it became known, it was all he could do to meet demand for his services.

He was twenty-three years old when Maria, bubbling with energy at nineteen, came to get her father's favourite rocking chair fixed. He liked her immediately and craftily took his time doing the simple repairs required, so that she had to make several visits to inquire on progress. To make his claim genuine, he deliberately broke some parts of the chair so that he could make new ones. This would take time, he told her.

They got married the week she turned twenty, by which time Solomon had a steady income from his furniture business and a local grinding mill that he had set up. He was thus able to pay the necessary *lobola* required to allow him to claim his wife and start a new life with her.

Four years and two kids later, they moved across town to a new residential area where Solomon built a modest home on the small piece of land that the local council was selling. Rather than relocate his grinding mill, Solomon opened another one. They were a simple couple with modest means. Grinding mills, while providing good income, did not generally bring in much profit in Solomon's new community. And most of his furniture customers were low-class workers who took things on credit. Solomon was content though, because the money that both his businesses brought in was enough to meet his family's basic needs, supplemented in a little way by Maria's token monthly salary after she found employment at the neighbourhood clinic as a nurse's aide.

They had five children. Solomon Jr, the eldest and only boy, was at university, studying for an accountancy degree. Anotida and Milagre were in their second and sixth years of high school respectively, and Demetria and Zvikomborero were still to complete their primary school. It was a very close knit and happy family, and the night of the arrival of Baby Chenzira (for that was the name they later gave her, meaning "of the street") resembled a low-key celebration.

Maria and Solomon did not go to the police in the end.

Zviko, ahead of Demetria, leaving for school the next morning, bumped and brushed past her sister shouting excitedly, "There's another one! Mommy, there's another one!"

Everyone rushed out. Zviko pointed at the small, grotesque bundle on the family veranda. It was a sad and pathetic sight. Wrapped in a dirty, worn, flimsy towel, the little boy looked malnourished. Once again Solomon wept openly as he gently picked it up and examined it, then passed it to his wife.

"What has got into people, *nhai Mwari*?" he asked, but God must have thought it a rhetorical question, for He did not answer.

A funereal atmosphere descended as, once again, the Manyika family crowded around their mother. This time, the excitement was replaced by fear, uncertainty and unanswered questions. Everyone trembled in harmony with the child's own shaking.

A crowd began gathering outside their gate. Unable to handle the curiosity, someone pushed the gate open and marched in, followed shortly thereafter by a wave of people pressing and shoving, all trying to get a look. They were all talking and shouting at once and, for fear of being crushed, Solomon led his family into the safety of their house, where he promptly locked all doors.

He went straight to the telephone and called the police. Perhaps hearing the commotion in the background, the local police arrived in less than ten minutes and restored order.

"What's going on, Mudhara Solo?"

Everyone in the area called Solomon Mudhara Solo. Chief Inspector Mwakutuya was the member-in-charge and had made the decision to lead his team himself to attend the scene. It was unheard of for Solomon Manyika to stir up trouble, and his instincts told him something must have happened.

Solomon narrated his story as Mwakutuya nodded along.

"Keep them for the time being," the officer said, finally, getting up. "Let me go and get social welfare."

He instructed two of his men to remain with the

family and left.

The girls refused to go to school and fussed over the children. The boy needed attention and there was fear that he might die. No one was sure how long he had been outside, exposed to the cold, with no food.

Chief Inspector Mwakutuya came back quite late in the afternoon, alone. He walked in, shaking his head and ignoring the salutes of his men.

Everyone looked at him. He sighed and shook his head again, then sat down on the nearest sofa. He bent forward and put his head between his hands. He remained like that for a while, and Solomon and Maria looked at each other in fear, then looked at the policeman as he slowly lifted his head and looked at them, his lips pursed.

"*Zvaramba*, it failed," he said, and shook his head once more. He looked like he was about to cry.

Solomon and his family just stared at him.

"We will try again tomorrow, but I was working social welfare the whole day," Mwakutuya said. "The people there are juniors. They seemed afraid to even come and see what we were talking about. They said they would have to wait until the bosses come who are at a workshop. I went back to my office and then returned. Twice I went there, but no luck. I don't know what's going on. We will try again tomorrow. Do you think…"

"We will cope," Maria said, and her husband nodded. "It's only for a while. We will keep them until they come."

***

"There are rules and protocols to follow, Mudhara Solo," the senior welfare officer said Saturday morning, a whole week later. "You can't just wake up one morning and say I want to look after orphaned and abandoned children."

"Exactly!" Solomon said. "That is why you are there, to tell me how to go about it. You people don't seem to have any capacity, and you don't seem to care either."

"Aaah Mudhara. You are insulting us now."

"How do you explain you only coming here a whole week after being told there were abandoned babies in the community?"

"It's not an insult, *mwanangu*," Maria piped in, with babies Chenzira and Masiiwa on either arm. "Don't tell me you're not seeing all those children roaming around on the streets. Whose children are they? What are you doing about it?"

"But *mhamha*, there is no way we can pick up every street kid. The state does not have the capacity nor the resources t…"

"Which is what this is about, isn't it? And may I correct you; don't call them street kids. The street does not give birth to human beings. They are lost and abandoned children roaming around, with nowhere to go, no one to look after them. They didn't choose this. Someone brought them into this world. They don't belong on the streets, they don't belong to the streets, and they are not street kids."

Solomon interjected before the welfare officer could reply. "We are not fighting. We are aware our government has so much on its hands and that resources are little. We are saying we want to help. *Chitibatsirai*, help us, so that we do our– "

"Mommy." They were interrupted by Ano.

Maria looked up. Her daughter was standing at the door, blocking from view someone standing behind her. She stepped aside and Mai Gwenzi, Maria's neighbour from two blocks down the road, stepped forward. She was holding a baby who seemed sound asleep.

Everyone got up.

"Oh my God!" The senior welfare officer was the first to speak.

"The boys found her in the banana plantation at the soccer field," Mai Gwenzi said. "My son came to tell me, and I immediately rushed there. It seems the person knew that since it's a Saturday, the boys will be playing soccer there. They wanted the baby found."

Maria kept staring at her neighbour. *Why is she bringing her here?*

Mai Gwenzi answered, as if she had heard, "You're the first person I thought of, Mai Solo. You know I am a widow and I struggle to even look after myself. I'm sorry Mai Solo."

Now everyone looked at the welfare officer. He sighed and sat down.

***

The paperwork to register the Manyikas' home as a halfway house for neglected and abandoned children did not take long, somehow tiptoeing its way through the bureaucracy and the bottlenecks. The only conditions they were given were to limit the number of children because of restricted space and that the children would have to leave when they attained legal age of majority.

Solomon Jr came from university to find his family home a buzz of little boys and girls of different ages, and a billboard at the gate identifying "Mumwe Mukana Halfway Home for Destitute Orphaned". Beneath it, in smaller but distinct, coloured type, it said, "Giving God's Children Another Chance." Mumwe Mukana. Another chance. As happens with long names, the community soon shortened it to just Mukana – The Chance. Solomon Jr felt a surge in his stomach. As he went into the house, he rubbed the heads of some of the little ones. When Milagre, the eldest of his sisters, had sent him a text message telling him what was happening, he had not at all pictured it like this. He wondered where they all fit.

He hugged both his parents, who were waiting anxiously when he walked in, fearful of what he might think and guilty that they had not waited to ask him, as the eldest and only boy.

"Thanks, mom. Thanks dad. I'm so proud of you," he said, much to their relief.

Immediately jumping to assist, Solomon Jr prevailed on a former classmate and close friend whose father worked for the town council and, within months, Mukana moved to the stables of an abandoned horse breeding project. There, the Manyikas set to work refurbishing the stables into habitable dormitories for the ever-increasing number of orphans.

The welfare officer was amazed at just how many seemed to be coming out of the woodwork and became an active weekend volunteer. Seeing the possibilities, and while completing a thesis on the problem of abandoned children for his social studies degree a year later, he resigned from his job and took up the post of the home's

Resident Superintendent. He had successfully convinced the philanthropist family that such a post would be a necessary and useful administrative function.

News travels fast and is lent wings when the press gets in on the act. The story of the Mukana Children's Home spread far and wide and soon, Solomon and Maria lost count of the number of media interviews they had to entertain. They went from ordinary, upper working-class peasants to community heroes virtually overnight. Donors streamed in and local non-governmental organisations came to offer assistance, while corporate businesses brought gifts – with journalists in tow. Solomon and Maria were grateful for all the help.

Then things changed.

***

Solomon Manyika Jr and his siblings are unable to pinpoint exactly where the problem started but can relate the sequence of events, as disjointed as they may be. Solomon Jr's body shakes when he narrates, "I am past angry now. I am only grateful that my parents played their part and showed the compassion that should form all our characters as human beings. They were not perfect, but then they were just simple, old citizens. They gave hopeless children another chance. You can't take that away from them. No one can."

Solomon Jr clears his throat, looks up, as if in deep thought, and continues, "I think, when you're a family running a business, there are certain things that you take for granted. All we wanted was to make sure our mom and dad succeeded, and we shared their vision. We did not even see it as a business. It was just us, the Manyika family, extending love to abandoned and helpless children, giving them another chance. We did not condemn. We did not judge. Our parents taught us that there are different reasons why people do the things they do, and that we needed to be thankful for, one, that they *abandoned* rather than *killed* their children and, two, they chose us – or God chose us, I don't know – to be that home of hope. When I say we took things for granted… all of us children got involved in the business, the calling. All of us. We did not consciously think in administrative terms, you know, like strategic long-term visions and plans, that kind of thing. Uh-uh. We loved all the children, we saw them as our little brothers and sisters, and I guess we thought that's all there was to it."

"When you say all of you got involved, what do you mean, exactly?" the reporter asks, his pen poised in mid-air. He takes a quick glance at his tape recorder.

"We were all workers and we were all members of the trustees board," Solomon Jr explains. "Even Ano and Deme, who were now working for other companies, they would be there on their days off."

"And you?"

"I quit my job for it. The pressure on my parents was too much and the money was reaching levels where they would not be able to cope. Father, remember, was only just a grinding mill owner and small-time furniture maker. Those things didn't bring in that kind of money, so this was different at all levels."

"What of your other sister, the eldest one, what's her name?"

"Mila. Milagre. It was the name of my father's

mother."

"Milagre," the reporter repeats, writing it down. "What happened to her? Where is she?"

"She's a software engineer for an IT company in Sierra Leone. Fortunately for her, most of this drama happened after she had already left."

"Why do you say, 'fortunately'?"

Solomon Jr smiles. "Father said she had his mother's temper. She would not have been able to handle it without a fight. She's quite the firebrand, and the whole country would have shaken with her noise and lawsuits. We made sure we only told her after everything."

"Ok, so all of you were board members. Were you looking at it like a family business?"

"Pretty much, I would say. The only person on the board who wasn't a family member was Persy."

"That's your Resident Supervisor? Percy as in P-E-R-C-Y? What's his full name?"

The reporter pauses and smiles at Solomon Jr's answer, then he scribbles it down and circles it.

"No, no, no. Perseverance. Perseverance Mwandibaya. Resident Superintendent."

"Unusual name," the reporter comments and asks, "What was the turning point?"

"So, we were at our management meeting. Persy was, for all practical purposes, our company adviser, and we had this routine of weekly management meetings, sometimes twice a week, then monthly and then a Board meeting every quarter. It was rather efficient, we thought. We trusted him big time. Anyway, at this management meeting…"

"Sorry to interrupt, when was this?"

"Oh, just about when we were getting into the second year of operations, which would be around March/April in the year of the takeover." Solomon Jr winces at the memory. He continues, slowly, reflectively, "In fact, I do remember that meeting, because it was on the anniversary of the day my family found Masiiwa. It was on April 6th. We call him our miracle baby. We made the day we found him his official birthday, but we did tell him he was probably a month or two older than that. Masiiwa means one who is left behind, abandoned. I'm sure you know that." The reporter responds with no more than a slight nod, and Solomon Jr continues. "So, Persy said an interesting proposal had come from an international NGO which was into the same mission as us, of looking after destitute children. They wanted to partner with us and, if we were interested, we would benefit from their international network, resources and training. As Resident Superintendent, he told us, he had agreed that their representatives visit the home the following week. And, indeed, they came; three white guys – a man and two women – and a black gentleman who was introduced as their programme officer in the Harare office. They came early in the morning, around nine and were there the whole day. We had to provide lunch and suspended our own programmes to entertain them. I'm mentioning this because it annoyed me and made me suspicious at the time. Persy had not mentioned they would be there for the entire day."

The reporter is curious and asks, "What were they doing the whole day? What time did they leave?"

"They left just after three. That's not the only thing that annoyed me. While we were having a discussion in dad's office, I took a break to go to the toilet and found one of the ladies talking to staff and some of our kids behind one of the dorms. I went where they were, and she quickly smiled and claimed she was just introducing herself and getting to know the place better. She had left and gone back to the meeting by the time I got out of the toilet. I told mom and dad my suspicions at supper that night. They all agreed it was suspicious, but the next day, when we asked him, Persy assured us that it was nothing, she was just being friendly. So, we let it go. A long time passed before we heard from them again."

"They came back after how long?"

"Four, five months. They didn't exactly come back, not in that manner. Persy relayed a message that Father was invited to a meeting with the international director of the NGO, who had arrived in Harare to assess their operations. Persy accompanied Father and I remained behind, overseeing things. Perhaps I should have gone with him."

"Why?"

"Father came back fuming and wouldn't eat. We had never seen him like that, and Mother said to let him be. It was only the next day that he told us what the director had said to him. Their assessment was that our project was too big for us and needed the intervention of professionals who know how to look after children…"

"No-oo!" The reporter is stunned. "Persy?"

Solomon Jr nods. "Father said he refused to talk to him all the way back, even when he tried explaining that it wasn't his doing, that they were working on reports from the team that had visited. But Persy sold himself out when he told Father he might like to think about what the director said and then…" Solomon Jr pauses. "…that sometimes it's good to divest oneself from emotional attachment, to let go when something becomes too big, let professionals take over! And that did it. Right the next day, we, as a family, fired Persy and asked him to leave immediately."

"Okay, okay, okay," the reporter says, "This is all so confusing. Why… no, what… okay, did the director… what was the NGO director insinuating?"

Solomon Jr gazes at the reporter for a while. "He wasn't insinuating. He made a direct offer to buy our family out of the project. Our own project!"

"What did your Father say?"

"What any right-thinking visionary would tell such vultures. He told them to go to hell."

There is some silence, Solomon Jr trying to calm his nerves as the memories threaten to choke him, and the reporter digesting what he's been told. Solomon Jr breaks the silence.

"They could have started their own," he says, and stares into space for another bout of silence. The reporter lets the silence prevail and waits. "Barely a month after we fired Persy," Solomon Jr finally sighs and continues, "we got a visit from government people in the social welfare ministry, saying they had come for an on-the-spot assessment of our home as they had received reports that children were being abused, forced to work in the gardens and to sweep the rooms, not getting enough to eat and some of them were not going to school. Further, that any staff member that dared raise concern was victimised, and that we had fired the resident superintendent because he had dared to suggest better ways of running Mukana."

"I remember stories written about that. How did you respond? Were these allegations totally false?"

Not for the first time, Solomon Jr regards his interviewer with interest. He says, after a brief pause, "You know, there is a way you can put a spin on facts that makes them sound ridiculous. You should know, right? Isn't that your job?"

The reporter smiles but does not answer.

"Growing up, our mom and dad taught us to work around the house and be self-reliant," Solomon Jr is speaking slowly now, squinted eyes gazing at some space through the open window. "Right now, no one can tell me what a clean house or yard looks like. I did that growing up. No one can teach me how to cook, or to sew, or to iron, wash clothes, weed the garden. I can do that. I grew up doing that. All my siblings are hard workers like that. That is why my sisters have been promoted ahead of their peers at their workplaces. Because of the sheer attitude and habit of hard work, honed from when they were babies. We all did manual work growing up. It was character forming, and now every single one of us can look after themselves. We did not see anything wrong with extending this philosophy to children we had adopted as an extended part of our family. They were not just children from the streets. They were family. Look at Masiiwa and Chenzira now, both of them exceptionally talented, both working for UN agencies and doing very well there. They grew up with us, doing what we did. The rest of those allegations, those are just outright lies, nothing else. No child ever failed to go to school. Staff were among the best paid.

Better paid than senior teachers in government schools, by far. I should know. I held the purse strings. I was the paymaster. Lies, all lies!" Solomon Jr stops, realising his chest is heaving with pent-up emotion. The reporter is nodding continuously.

Solomon Jr recounts how the entire matter affected his father's health, how the pressure mounted and how, one fine, cool and quiet morning, on a day when all the siblings were sitting outside, soaking up the early morning sun, their mother came out of the house, shuffling her feet, dazed and confused. She suddenly let out a loud and long wail, calling out to her long-gone mother, spun around and collapsed to the ground, unconscious. When Ano ran into the house to tell Father, she found him still, cold and motionless on their bed and let out her own wild, hysterical scream. Reacting to the pandemonium, some neighbours had the presence of mind to rush their mother to the clinic, where she was restored to consciousness. She had suffered a bad stroke, and afterwards, she was incoherent for months.

After they buried their father, their mother would not step anywhere near the orphanage. Milagre was unable to attend the funeral as she had travelled overseas, where she grieved alone.

Solomon Jr tells the reporter that he then called the international NGO and told them he was ready to talk.

"They came, almost too quickly, as if they were expecting my call. We signed the papers that bought us out completely. They had their lawyers. We didn't need any. That international director was there, all patronising and triumphant grin. I remember what he said after we signed. 'You did a good job. Children are the future, and they need special care. So, thank you, we will take it from here, and you won't regret it.' He wanted to shake hands, but I just walked out. My sisters and I took a long walk around the complex, saying goodbye to our little brothers and sisters. Do you know how that feels? We were probably never going to see them again. They have forgotten now, of course. They were babies. There's nothing at that new place that even acknowledges what my parents did. Nothing."

Solomon Jr's voice trails off.

The reporter stares at him for a while, then asks, "Why did you do it? Why did you not fight? This was your project, your parents' vision!"

Solomon Jr looks at him the way someone looks at a madman, with amused sympathy. After a while, he concludes his deliberation, "Two reasons. First, we knew we couldn't win against the powerful forces facing us… that fight was futile. Of course, Mila would have done it for principle's sake. But we didn't have it in us, the rest of us. We had lost the spirit to fight. Secondly, that project killed my father and made my mother go crazy in the head; I don't think any of us could have handled the trauma, walking around that complex. It was best to let it go."

Almost as if scared to ask, the reporter whispers his last question, "What about your mother, what happened to her?"

Solomon Jr looks into the far distance again, then smiles wistfully. "Ah, Mai Maria. Dear old Mother Mary. That's what everyone called her. Mai Maria. She never fully recovered her faculties, you know. So…" his voice breaks as he continues, "she drank poison. We found her dead in her room, sitting on the edge of her bed with her chin on her chest like this, holding her husband's picture. She was smiling. And this time, Milagre came. Milagre came. Closure, you know."

***

The long blurb introducing the reporter's feature story that weekend read: *This children's home is one with lots of sentimental emotion. But no one remembers its origins or history. What you see is not its original name. Its name was changed at the whim of new owners who took it by subtle force, foreigners who are teaching African children their ways and values. No one remembers its founders, simple peasants in a small community who only answered a call to care, when no one else did. No one remembers, except the founder's children. No one remembers, because all history has been obliterated and any news reports ever written about it are, for some reason, not available anymore, not even on the internet. No one remembers, but will you, after reading this?*

TAMARA

FOR the 36-year-old man sitting by the roadside, the playful little girl from up the road looked more and more like a woman these days. Those little breasts were beginning to sprout like ripe fruit, firm and round. Before long, he thought, she would be wearing a bra.

He watched her as she skipped and danced along the road on her way home from school, her satchel slung over her back; she was in high spirits again. She was always in high spirits. And, as usual, she was singing as she pranced along like a playful little puppy.

Tamara. He smiled as he sat idly by the roadside culvert, watching her. They said she was bright in school. No wonder she was happy and playful. She had nothing to worry about. She certainly had a good upbringing, caring parents. He envied them. He envied her. He wished his wife had given him at least one Tamara, naturally beautiful like a flower, pretty like a picture. But alas, eleven years of marriage had yielded nothing. He yearned for a child. He yearned for a Tamara.

They had tried everything. Modern medicine failed at the first hurdle. The doctors just did not have any explanation for it. All the tests had shown no evidence of a problem on the part of either of them. The traditional healers were a waste of time and money, but the couple only realised this after visiting a seventh one. Godobori had at least been honest; the spirits were flabbergasted by this one, he pronounced, after casting his bones several times and shaking his head each time in total puzzlement. He declined payment and advised them to keep trying, perhaps to try and relax when they came together. The hunter, he said, the hunter knows that just as he is about to give up after a tiring expedition, that is when the spirits of the forest decide to reward him for his perseverance. Persevere, my son, persevere, my daughter, the spirits will reward you. But there were tears of pity and helplessness in Godobori's eyes when he dismissed them and watched them leave. If they had looked back, they would have seen him shake his head in sadness.

Then they went to the missionaries. After numerous prayer sessions involving the whole congregation, they gave up and stopped going to church. What kind of God is it who, for a whole two years, refuses to listen to the plaintive cries of a whole congregation? Was a single child, of any sex, too much to ask for, or was that kind of benevolence reserved for Abram and Sarai alone?

His face clouded. He frowned and thought about his wife, about the curse that had befallen them. What was it? Where did all this come from? Everybody else in the family had children. His elder brother had five. His younger brother immediately after him had nine that he could barely look after. One of his elder brother's sons who was now in high school had even impregnated a classmate. He felt small. His wife's four sisters had between them eleven children. And his cousin, Tamara's father, had a girl and a boy. Everybody had offspring to show off. Yet he and his wife had not managed even a stillbirth. He had stopped blaming his wife. It had, once upon a time, got to a point where they fought about it, where each one suspected the other of barrenness, but that had passed. Still, the reality was too much to accept. The tension in the house was increasingly becoming unbearable.

"Good afternoon, uncle. Are you not feeling well?"

Tamara!

He had all but forgotten her in his reverie and sat up with a start. The grin that came to his face was involuntary.

"Ah, Tamara. No, daughter of my brother. I am perfectly well. It is just that I am deep in thought and…"

"Eeh uncle. What kind of thoughts could they be that make a grown man like you so blind that you do not even notice your own daughter?"

Eh, eh. Listen to her thinking and talking like a grown woman already. He smiled at her and beckoned, "Come and sit here beside me and tell me about your health and about school. You are one of the brightest kids in school, I hear? Come, sit."

He did not expect her to decline his invitation and was taken aback when she did. His pride was stung by her refusal.

"No, uncle," she said ever so sweetly, "I must run home. Mother says I have to help in the house. And I want to get there before Tawanda. Besides, teacher gave us a lot of homework today."

"In that case," he offered, recovering quickly, "let me walk you home and we can talk as we walk."

She laughed. She let him carry her school bag when he offered, which made him happy again. As they walked towards her home up the road, he found himself telling her stories about his own school days. She applauded each little tale with genuine laughter and he, in turn, glowed with pride, happy to be having this effect on her. Oh, how he longed for a child who he could tell stories about his own childhood. He pushed that thought aside before it had a chance to depress him again and told her the story of the day they scared the domestic science teacher with a rubber snake and how, when she fainted, they were all sent on punishment to the school gardens and ended up stealing the peas. She laughed heartily, saying he must have been a very naughty pupil.

Her house came up. The house itself was as ordinary as all the others in the middle-class suburb, but what set it apart was its well-trimmed outside lawn, complemented by a colourful cornucopia of various bright flowers in bloom. Passers-by could not help but gawk as they walked past and some stole quick photoshoots on the lawn. It looked more alive than all the others, although most of them were virtually the same design and size, a veritable architect's nightmare and the result of a bank's housing scheme. Tamara's parents had managed to make theirs look different.

He did not want to get up to the house. He was too envious and ashamed. He knew it was not their fault that he was in the situation he was. It was just that, well, they seemed to have everything and everything seemed to work for them: a beautiful house, good jobs, beautiful children… Children!

Rather sadly, he said goodbye to Tamara, and said that he had to turn back. That mother of hers would not allow him to go home once she saw him, what with her love for stories, he explained weakly in a desperate attempt at light-heartedness. She rewarded him with one of her laughs. This time it seemed mocking. He turned away quickly so that she could not see his pained face.

Tamara.

He thought about her and the children he could not have as he walked back towards his house. *If I had children*, he told himself, *I would send them to the best schools in the land. They would not want for anything. They would grow up big and strong and healthy and intelligent and beautiful, just like Tamara. They would have good clothes and toys and things, mountains of things. They would laugh and sing and dance and be happy, just like Tamara.*

His mind envisioned him in another world, only different from this one because in it, he had children. He pictured himself in all sorts of happy situations with his children, buying them popcorn and pizza and ice cream and taking them on joy rides, pampering them no end and being envied by his neighbours because he was such a contented man with beautiful, bright children whom he knew how to look after. This last thought depressed him as he told himself that he was just but dreaming.

Tamara.

Suddenly he hated her. He hated her and all that she represented. He hated her for reminding him of his impotence. He hated her for… for being there. An unexplained fury suddenly overcame and engulfed him so that, inexplicably, he started to walk faster. He picked up a loose stone and flung it aimlessly in front of him. It hit a tree trunk and ricocheted back in his direction, losing momentum and dropping some distance ahead of him. He followed it and kicked it into the roadside. He came upon his favourite culvert, the one he always sat on to watch Tamara coming home from school. Suddenly, he felt tired. He sat down and, leaning forward, buried his face in his hands. He was like that for what seemed an eternity. Had someone passed by, they would have noticed that when he raised his head, his eyes were red, swollen and wet. The big man had been crying softly, overcome by emotion and self-pity.

"Oh, Tamara," he mumbled under his breath, surprising himself.

Now he did not feel like going home anymore. He knew that if he did, he would almost certainly start a fight with his wife. He set off in the direction of the emergency taxi rank where he boarded a car that would take him to the high-density suburb where he had spent his childhood. This was where he was born, where he grew up, where he went to school, where he had found his wife, where he had had his first lodgings and then later, where he had bought a small house which they later sold to raise the deposit for the middle-density house where they now lived. This township, this is where he had his roots. The rural home meant very little to him. He had tried, and failed, to stay there. The rural home and him had nothing in common. He could not identify with it. He could not relate. He made the occasional trips to visit the old folk, but those trips lasted just a day, if even that. The old folk never had anything to say to him except to address the thorny, embarrassing and humiliating issue of his failure to give them grandchildren, like his siblings. Even if they were discussing plantings or harvests, they would somehow find a way of smuggling the subject in. "Now, if I had more grandchildren, we could plant this vast field in no time at all!" He didn't like going home, and only went because he had to. But this township, this was his home. He felt lightheaded as he disembarked from the taxi.

You can take me out of the ghetto
And then never take me back again
But you will never take the ghetto
Out of meeeee!

The Oliver Mutukudzi refrain came to his head and found its way past his vocal cords, unbidden.

He headed for Marengenya, the local pub whose name translates to tattered clothes.

***

Tamara spoke to Sisi, the maidservant, about her uncle. Sisi was a quiet, elderly woman, older than Tamara's mother, although she called the younger woman "mama" like the children did. She was herself quite the lovable sort, but the problem was she spoke very little, and then, only when she was spoken to.

"Just be careful with that uncle of yours, Tamara," she said. "I don't trust him."

Tamara was surprised. How could anyone say that of such a sweet, harmless old man?

155

"Why do you say that?"

"Eeh," said Sisi rather cryptically, and left it at that to concentrate on wiping a plate.

Tamara knew Sisi well enough to know the subject was closed. She hummed a tune as she helped with the dishes. But her mind kept thinking about Uncle. He seemed to be in some sort of trouble. A person could not just spend the whole day sitting by a roadside bridge with a faraway look in his eyes, talking to himself. They had to be thinking deeply about something. Was he fighting with Aunty? Maybe it had to do with their lack of children. She knew a little about that. Mother and Father had talked about it when they thought the children were out of earshot. But Tamara and Tawanda were sitting on the veranda, out of view, and they had heard. A lot of the phrases they used were strange, words that Tamara, let alone little Tawanda, had not heard before, and language they were not even taught at school. Shona was such a funny language. They only taught you certain things at school but there was a kind of old people talk that you never learnt. They always seemed to be talking in parables and incomplete sentences and one had to be pretty clever to deduce the meaning.

Tawanda had wanted to ask, the silly boy. Tamara admonished him strongly and stopped him, reminding him that he was not supposed to have heard anything in the first place and would be beaten up badly by Father for eavesdropping on the conversation of adults. But one day she would ask, she resolved, one day she would find a way to ask. She felt pity for uncle and wished she could help.

She was eleven years old now. She had a long, smooth face with high cheekbones. Her small slits of eyes were always smiling. Her jet-black hair was set in the ponytail schoolgirl fashion of the moment. Her father said it was too long and should be cut, but her mother preferred to keep it in braids and had won the argument. Tamara herself couldn't care less and would have agreed with her father because short hair was easier to look after, but she had no say in the matter. She had an athlete's body and kept it trim by taking active part in all manner of school sports. She had a sharp mind and picked things up quickly and easily. People said she was a gifted child and very mature for her age. Her father often teased her mother by declaring that she took after him. On her part, Mother would just give him a sly look from the corner of her eye, smile and say nothing.

Tamara worked mechanically. A plate slipped from her hands and dropped into the sink, jolting her back to reality. Luckily it did not break. Sisi, who was staring at her, shook her head and looked away.

Finally, the dishes were done. Tamara went to her room to do her homework, but she could not concentrate. She stared at her books, seeing visions of her uncle on the culvert, out-of-focus face contorted by painful thoughts. As she watched, his body levitated. He seemed to be floating without going anywhere, just drifting around the same place in the gravity-defying trick he had conjured, perhaps for Tamara's benefit.

Tawanda, who had had afternoon sports, came home about the same time as her parents. They walked into the house just as he let out a screech of laughter which startled his sister awake. She looked about her in sleep-induced confusion, rubbing her eyes. She wondered at what point she had fallen asleep.

She was sweating, she noticed. She was sweating and breathing heavily from all that running in the dream. Strange dream: Her uncle had been walking her home in much the same way as he had when she returned from school earlier. As usual, he was full of stories, and she was laughing gaily at all his little tales. It was not strange in the dream that they seemed to be floating as they walked, or that the road kept going on and on, even moving and dragging them along as if it was a conveyor belt. The road then suddenly dissolved out of sight after offloading them onto the middle of a lovely green forest, full of *musasa* and eucalyptus and pine and all the beautiful trees in the world. Some of them looked like they were growing upside down, with their roots in the sky. Many had climbers twisting around them in a merry dance, and the birds, bees, butterflies and little forest animals helped themselves to an endless choice of fruits and berries and pollen. She liked the strong climbers that wound themselves around the trees and thought they were particularly clever. Uncle said some of them could choke the trees and take over, making them twist and turn as they rose into the sky.

The grass was as soft and comfortable as a deep pile carpet. The leaves, when they fell in the cool breeze, had a lovely feel when they touched her bare arms and cheeks. The light of the bright sun danced merrily between the trees and Tamara felt as if she was in Paradise. She challenged her uncle to a game in which they chased and caught butterflies. The one with the largest collection of the most beautiful butterflies was the winner. Uncle let her win, and they had lots of fun releasing the butterflies and watching them fly off in lovely friezes of colour.

Afterwards, she started dancing. Uncle's laughter rang out with appreciation and encouragement, and he clapped for her, making her more creative with her dancing. Now she was dancing for him because she liked to hear his laughter. She liked to make him happy. She started going round and round in circles, swaying and swinging and dancing and singing until she could no longer hear him. At one point, when she opened her eyes, she saw him sitting cross-legged on the ground, watching her with his arms folded on his knees, chin resting on his arms and a smile in his eyes. Tamara danced and danced like a ballet dancer until she dropped to the ground, tired but laughing all the while.

At last, she stopped laughing and immediately thought something had gone wrong. Why was Uncle not coming to lift her up in his powerful arms? She sat up and looked around. He was not there! She got up and called for him, but he did not answer. She called and called again, but the only sound she heard was the whispering of the wind in the forest. She looked around wildly and realised she did not know where she was. It had become a quiet forest, with no birds, no bees, no butterflies, no little forest animals – just a dark, silent eeriness and an ominous whistling wind.

Suddenly Tamara was afraid. She started running. She did not plan which direction to go, she just ran. On and on she ran. The forest seemed to have no end. Several times, she fell, tripping over large tree roots protruding from the earth. Each time, she got up, gathered her skirts

and started running again. When it seemed like she had
been running forever, and she was too tired to go any
further, she sat on a rock. Then she heard voices. She
strained her ears to try to determine where they were
coming from, but she could not. She tried to call out,
but she was too tired. Suddenly, from somewhere above
her head, a loud screech of laughter made her jump out
of her skin.

Tamara rubbed her eyes again. Stupid Tawanda! He
was laughing at her for sleeping in the daytime. Did he
always have to laugh so loud? As she stretched to go and
greet her parents who she could hear in the kitchen, she
wondered about the dream and about her uncle. She had
only one question troubling her: why had he abandoned
her in the forest on her own? That was very
uncharacteristic of him.

***

Uncle got so drunk at Marengenya, the place of the
tattered souls, that the barman, an old friend, pitied him
and dragged him into the drinks warehouse. He dumped
him there, covered him with an old blanket and the
drunken man promptly started snoring among the cases
of beer bottles.

When he returned an hour before opening time the
next morning, the barman found him still fast asleep.
After contemplating him for a while, the barman went
back and fetched a jug of water from the bar fridge. He
poured a steady stream of the ice-cold water on the
sleeping man's forehead and drew an immediate sharp
reaction.

His wife was sitting in the kitchen when he got home, cupping a mug of tea with both hands and staring into space. She looked at him without expression as he shuffled through the door. She kept eyeing him as he pulled a chair and sat down. She watched him closely, her eyes not missing anything. He looked tired and haggard. He kept his eyes down, guilt and shame written all over his face. A soft sigh escaped his lips as he sat. His breath smelt foul. Stale beer, she thought. He's been drinking again.

After what seemed an eternity, he looked up and opened his mouth to speak. She got up and left the room.

A few minutes later she was back, all dressed up. It was simple dressing, with a long and loose-fitting dress, soft hues of the colour blue on a polka dot design. She wore flat black shoes, as if to emphasise her lack of height. Her face was untouched by makeup and her hair was braided in simple cornrows. Even now, one would readily admit she was a natural beauty, her light features accentuating a well-proportioned body. But there was something else that seemed to take away from all this – a pained and perpetually thoughtful expression, as if she might start crying anytime.

"I am going to town to pay the bills," she said without stopping, adjusting her handbag and walking briskly past her husband and out the door.

He watched that door for a long time after she had left and then got up wearily. She had left some food for him, as usual. In her own way, she still loved him, and he knew that only this thing, which he dared not mention out loud, got in their way. If only the gods would answer their prayers, they would be a happy couple again.

He realised how hungry he was when he finished eating and found he still wanted more. He cleaned up the plates, tidied the kitchen and went to the bathroom where he took a long, cold shower.

The knocking got louder and louder. He heard it as soon as he turned off the shower. Whoever it was must have been knocking for some time. He shouted that he would be out soon, and the knocking stopped. He dried himself and dressed quickly, wondering who it could be. They hardly got visitors these days and suspected people were avoiding them as if they were carrying The Virus. It made them feel even worse. If only the gods… He shook his head again and went to open the door.

Tamara!

She stood there in all her innocence. She smiled sweetly at him, and he gasped before he could catch himself. His head spun in confusion and excitement. He wanted to smile but he could not. He just stood, thunderstruck, staring as if he had seen an apparition.

"What's the matter, uncle?" she cooed, and his stomach did unexplainable somersaults. "You look like you've seen a ghost. Are you going to let me in?"

He recovered. "Tamara, my daughter. You must forgive me. I didn't expect you… I was taking a bath… You're the last person… Ah, this hangover… Come in, come in, what a pleasant surprise."

He stepped aside to let her pass. She walked in confidently, with the familiar air of one who knew her surroundings. She went straight to the sitting room and threw herself carelessly on a sofa. She looked around, got up and went to the radio, switched it on and said,

"Grown-ups! How can you stay in such a quiet house? Where's Aunty?"

Before he could answer, she was shouting, "Aunty! Aunty!"

"She's just gone to town. You missed her by a few minutes," he eventually managed to say.

"In that case," she said, "I am leaving. I came to see Aunty, Mother sent me. When she comes back, please tell her…"

He felt a deep sinking feeling and protested. He moved in to stop her leaving.

"No, no, no, no! Don't go. Please, stay and, and, and… and have a drink or something. Do you want a drink?"

She declined his offer and insisted she had to go. She tried to walk past him, but he blocked her way. This puzzled her, and she stopped and looked at him quizzically. Her face registered confusion, which slowly and progressively degenerated to fear as she saw the strange, leering expression on his face.

"Uncle?" she said, her voice trembling in a hoarse, frightened whisper.

He did not answer. He kept standing there, now breathing heavily, and his eyes opened wider as he advanced towards her, and she slowly backed away. And then everything went wild before she blacked out.

***

When she eventually opened her eyes, they were painful, and she could not see properly. She was only able to make out the blurry images of her mother and father, each holding either of her hands. Father looked helpless and his attempt to smile at her failed. He started shaking, then broke into uncontrolled sobbing. Mother sniffled, her nose dribbled, and she wiped tears from her eyes with her free hand.

Tamara tried to talk but no sound came from her. She had so many questions. After several attempts, she gave up and drifted off to an uneasy sleep in which she dreamt of the forest again…

CHIKWATA FROM 6POUNDS

IT would have been funny had it not been so worrisome, the way it happened. Jairos' version was that it was Arthur who first came up with the idea and, being the type who didn't like to be questioned, the others went along with it rather than get into his bad books. Arthur's version, on the other hand, was that they forced him into it when he told them what he had seen at the white man's house. Not wanting to lose their friendship, he had played along but had his doubts from the beginning, since it was not anything they were familiar with.

The one thing they now agreed on was it was dangerous to try something you have never tried before, especially when there was no one to teach you.

"Arthur does not want anyone arguing with him," says Jairos. "He always wants it his way and, since he's always the one with the money, we have no choice."

Money for what?

To buy sweets, to go to the local bioscope, to buy ice cream, to pay for the "money game" and slug and to watch the weekend match at Gwanzura Stadium, especially when Black Aces are playing.

But where does Arthur get all that money?

His father is a doctor, and his mother is a nurse. And there are only three in their family. In fact, two, because the third is not Arthur's sister, *sister*. His father only adopted her when his brother died, and her mother married another man. She was an only child. Arthur has only one sister, who comes after him. We are not allowed to say this, says Jairos, so we just pretend that he has two sisters when everyone knows the truth. Also, the children of your father or mother's brothers and sisters are your brothers and sisters too. This is only confusing if you are a white person who believes in cousins. We have no "cousins" in our culture. Anyway, Arthur and his sisters always have pocket money, lots of it. So much in fact that they do not even know what to do with it. Jairos reveals what Vinnie said, that Arthur uses this money to buy the friendship of *Chikwata*, the gang, otherwise he would not have any friends.

Jairos is such a gossip, says Maglobo who has eyes as big as light bulbs sitting beneath his forehead under two forests of jet-black eyebrows. Maglobo looks comical with his small nose and incomplete lips. It's very embarrassing for a man to love talking about everything, he says. What will the girls do?

Jairos says the idea came to Arthur after his dad took them to visit one of his white friends *kuma-yard*, exclusively white zones where one family's yard could swallow the whole of the "6Pounds" houses where *Chikwata* lived. Why were they called 6 Pounds? An unverified claim was that the rentals here, at six pounds per month, distinguished in class the residents here from the rest of the "African township" people. What about "12 Pounds" – were those even better? Maglobo and Jairos look at each other, then at Vinnie, and they all shrug.

"It doesn't matter," Maglobo ventures at last. "We are all in the gutter, unlike where Arthur went."

He has spoken a wisdom not expected for a child his age and everyone goes silent, thinking about where Arthur had gone, what he had seen. There was a certain affectedness about Arthur when he came back from that visit, and he was up very early the next morning, waking everyone to play, but really, he wanted to boast about his experience. Being close to white people and playing with their children was not something you did every day. Hey, speaking English itself was scary! But Arthur spent a whole afternoon speaking and *playing* in English! Arthur earned and deserved his bragging rights.

They squatted together in a huddle – Arthur, Maglobo, Jairos, Vinnie, Twoboy (whose twin brother, because he came out first, was called Bigboy but was not in this gang) and Success – as Arthur dramatically outlined the new venture as if he was talking about a big project investment. This is where the versions differ: Arthur argues that he was describing what he had seen, and his friends got excited and convinced him to try it!

Two days later, they were staring up the big avocado pear tree at Arthur's house, one of a handful of exclusive houses in a separate section of their own, away from the ordinary houses of the township. These houses belonged to comparatively much richer families – businesspeople, doctors and lawyers, engineers, university lecturers, senior rank policemen and black nationalist politicians – who were yet to be allowed to reside in the white man's "yards", although they could afford it.

It was nice and cool and shady in this part of the yard at Arthur's house. The first time Arthur had brought them to show them the orchard at the back, with its trees of mango and apple and peach and orange and "English maize", a misnomer for pomegranates, he had stood akimbo, crossed his arms and smirked as they stood there, awestruck to open-mouthed speechlessness. The short pathway leading to it was bordered either side by well-trimmed rose bushes splashing out more colours than a rainbow during a monkey's wedding. They all breathed in the sweet scent and sucked in the opulence, wondering where their parents had been when God was dishing out talents and making some people rich.

Here at the back, too, was a neat veranda on a raised platform, complete with wooden rails, a cushioned rocking bamboo chair and a swinging bench-for-three hanging solidly by steel chain from the rafters above. It was way cooler than the swings at the CJ Hall playground, which squeaked discordantly on unoiled hinges. Those CJ contraptions were frightening, just looking at them. There were two in particular, hanging precariously and tilting at a distorted angle, one side much shorter than the other, such that everyone wondered whether it was some kind of engineering fail or the works of a sociopath with a twisted sense of humour. Once upon a time, Success, who has the unfortunate distinction of getting into mishaps, got so excited swinging here (not on the engineering-challenged ones, thank God) that he went too high – *whee-eee, whee-eee!* – and somehow managed to go an entire 360 degrees, not once, but twice, and wound his chain around the crossbar as he went over it! As he threatened to go a third time, his panic got the better of him and he jumped off, earning himself some painful adventure bruises from the pebbles in the patch of dry sand where he rolled and lay still as if unconscious. He did not die, but maintained he came dangerously close.

The swing at Arthur's house wouldn't do that. This one "had gone to private school", *Chikwata* agreed. It had lovely oblong maroon cushions on the two ends to complement the longer grey one to sit on, and it was a proud Arthur that told *Chikwata* the bench was made of teak. Not having any idea what teak was, they concluded that it must be some kind of expensive wood, the way Arthur made the revelation. It certainly looked that way but then, so did everything else at this house. A few neatly sited baskets of drooping plants completed the eye candy, but *Chikwata* collectively wondered whether the doctor and his nurse wife ever found time to sit here, contemplate the world and count their blessings, given their work schedules. Of Arthur, there was no question: it would have been surprising if he had even stepped onto that veranda, as he was always coming to the 6Pounds to seek companionship when he wasn't at school. The girls, maybe, but judging from the veranda's cleanliness, it seemed Sisi Maka, the house help, was the only one who played here.

"How do we get up there?" Vinnie wanted to know as

the boys contemplated the tree. "And how do we get all
the stuff up?"

"Easy," said Arthur, "one of us climbs up, and then
we tie the wood and everything we need onto a rope,
and he can pull it up."

There was some hesitation as they all looked up again,
with some misgivings. Arthur ran off and soon came
back struggling with a long ladder. They helped him with
it and leant it against the imposing tree, whose little
green oval-shaped fruits were growing steadily firmer by
the day. It was the season. Arthur ran off again and
returned with a thick rope hanging from his left shoulder
into the crook of his arm. It must have been heavy, for
he staggered with this load as well and, as if to confirm
so, he threw it to the ground in relief. Still the boys
looked at him and waited.

"You go up," Twoboy said with some authority to
Arthur. "Success, go with him *sha*."

Success looked sceptical, but everyone else pretended
not to notice as they squinted their eyes at the tree in
exaggerated concentration. Since there was no argument,
the two climbed steadily up the ladder and were soon at
the solid lowermost branches of the avocado tree. Now it
was time to send up the building materials and working
tools.

What they should have done first, Jairos reasons later,
is they should have carried the smaller items like the
hammer and the nails first. And they should have tied
ropes around their waists. What difference would that
have made, Vinnie counters, obviously not appreciating
the value of such a statement of Jairos's convictions.
Jairos, of course, always comes up with these wayward

remarks sometimes unrelated to the subject at hand and the boys just look at him, only responding if it's too ridiculous. They think if he remains quiet for too long, his lips might clamp and stick together, therefore he has to say something all the time regardless of whether it makes sense or not.

"Guys," Success shouted down from the tree, "should we not have a design first? I mean, how do we build without a plan?"

"But I told you yest… on Wednesday!" Arthur shouted back. "It's not that difficult. Mudhara Spickles did the sketches. We know what we want, and we have the materials, so let's build. We are wasting time talking!"

The two of them are up there, perched precariously on the same branch, next to each other and yet they are shouting, Jairos recalls and gets caught up in his own laughter.

Arthur had, the day before, gone to see Old Spickles, the furniture man at The Stones shopping centre, and asked for his help. They just called him 'Old' but he was only around forty-two years old; it's just that he seemed to take a bath only once a month. It was hard to find anyone who knew his real name. Township legend in Highfield was that he was explaining some bill of quantities for a coloured guy who said he wanted to build a toolshed at the house he had moved into a month earlier, right there in 6Pounds. "You'll need lots of three-quarter spickles. I don't tell you how many, lots, you'll just see." He meant nails but since he was speaking in English and forgot the correct word, he just anglicised the Shona word for nails, which is *zvipikiri*. From then on, people teased him and called him Spickles and it stuck, leaving only those who really knew him from back then that could recall his actual name to say it when necessary, which was almost never.

Now, pleased and feeling honoured to have the company of the doctor's son in his workshop, Old Spickles tried to sell him all the stuff he needed and other stuff he didn't, just so he could get rid of it. Business was low that week and had been for almost the whole month now. Joao Echo the Moscan, his Mozambican and Muslim friend who ran the barbershop adjacent to Spickles' workshop, teased him that he should learn to not make furniture that did not break.

They said of Joao that he spoke with an echo, on account of his tendency to repeat some of the words he said, as if to emphasise the key points.

"Look at this chair you made for me, for example. People of all shapes and sizes have been sitting on it for the past ten years, yet it doesn't even creak to this day, not a sound, and too much comfort! Ten years! Not a sound! How many times has Big Sam sat on it? Big Sam! Everything he sits on breaks but in this chair, he met his match! Met his match!" And Joao Echo would rock himself in laughter, tap the side of his head with two fingers and tell Spickles to have a better business mind.

Old Spickles listened attentively with his face the frown of Socrates the thinker-philosopher, looking far away and nodding thoughtfully in agreement, as young Arthur explained his project. He soon retired to the back of his workshop, to his warehouse, and was back there for a good twenty minutes. When he came out, it was with the following materials:

*1.	2x8' lengths of 2x8 timber (should have been treated but weren't)*
*2.	6x8' lengths of 2x6 timber, also untreated*
*3.	3x10' lengths of 2x4 timber, untreated*
*4.	6x12' lengths of 1x6 decking material*
*5.	3x10" long ¾ lag screws and washers*
*6.	8 galvanised rafter ties*
*7.	1 bagful of nails and deck screws.*

That was all.

"What do you mean, that's all?" Maglobo was the first to express his doubts. He thought it was too much. "Are you sure we can do this? This is so much stuff," he voiced and immediately regretted it.

"Go home if you don't want," Arthur said testily. "Or go and play *mahumbwe* with my sisters back there."

No one said anything after that.

Arthur had found and paid off a local boy with a pushcart to carry his stuff home and put it all in the tool shed. When he brought it out on the day of 'the assignment', he also took out some boards and old timber – treated, funny enough – left over from when his father had had Sekuru Mafios, the gardener, fence off the vegetable garden. He also brought out some of his father's tools: a hammer, a table saw, a power drill and tape measure.

"We make the deck first," Arthur said, but appeared doubtful. He inclined his head to one side then the other, trying to figure out the sketch drawn with blue ballpoint pen on the back of used cardboard. He was trying to remember what Old Spickles had told him. He turned the cardboard around, but it only served to confuse him more.

"Uhm, shouldn't we…?" Vinnie started to ask but went quiet.

There should have been another tree nearby, that's what I read in a carpentry book, says Jairos, wiser after the event.

But remember, Maglobo counters, we changed that and agreed we could build on that one tree, it was big enough.

This was true. The avocado pear tree had a big bough that tapered off to the right, as if one trunk was troubled by the straight, upward trajectory and decided to veer off in its own direction.

Trouble was, not being experts at either woodwork or any kind of DIY handywork, the boys were totally at sea and, in the end, started hammering wood and nails all over the place in their effort to construct a house on the branches of a tree. It was a disaster.

If it was just a disaster, it would have been alright. The unmitigatedness of the disaster was in a class of its own, and by the end of the day, three of the boys had earned unsolicited tattoos deep enough to last their lifetimes. Funny enough, Arthur, who ought to have come off the worst from the heavy impact of his flying descent and landing, only had minor scratches and a sore back that lasted just a week.

It is more than possible that the version of events benefits from new, enriching facts at each subsequent telling, as each member of *Chikwata* recalls something forgotten during the most recent recounting. Today's version will, therefore, have to do.

The first indication that things would go wrong,

recalls Vinnie, was when Success got his shoe stuck between some branches, and the more he tried to free himself, the more stuck he got. He kept cursing… Vinnie is fingering the small bump on the left side of his face, remnants of a healed scar.

Arthur and Success had moved a couple of branches up the tree so they could work better on the branches below, where the deck of their tree house would sit. If such reasoning confounded any of their comrades below, none dared to voice their concern.

Success explains that he was trying to reach across to Arthur to hand over to him the hammer and nails. When he tried to adjust his footing so that he could extend his reach, he found that his right leg had somehow got stuck between the two sturdy branches he had used as vice grips to stabilise himself.

Arthur, in turn, decided to reach out to Success and lend a hand. Unfortunately, the branch he chose to support himself on was only a twig that had seen better days and had dried. He leaned on it too hard, and it snapped with a loud crack before he inevitably lost his footing.

What followed was a scene of flailing arms, flying implements, breaking branches, little grenades of hard, green, unripe fruit and leaves, and falling, wailing bodies. Arthur dived into freefall, crashed into his buddy whose foot decided at that crucial moment that it did not need the shoe covering it and bequeathed it to the branches, which, thus pacified, let Success go and watched him careering down through the rest of the tree with Arthur not far behind. Twoboy, who had been lounging on the ladder, turned and looked up in panic and, in his haste to escape, tripped on the ladder, which left its position against the tree and followed him. It caught up with him not long after and crashed into his back, sending him tumbling to the floor. Seconds later, a double thud announced the arrival onto that same earthy tarmac, of Arthur and Success, the former being cushioned in his fall by the latter.

Jairos, Maglobo and Vinnie were rooted to their spot just beneath the veranda, open-mouthed, wide-eyed and clasping hands behind their heads. Later, they were unable to explain how they got to the veranda when, not so long before, they had been standing under the avocado pear tree. Vinnie deduced that the hard avocado pear that hit him on the side of his face and scarred it must have assisted his flight to safety.

Arthur rolled off Success and groaned, feeling a sore back. Suddenly, he asked, "Whose blood is that?"

But there were two sets of blood in the sand. One belonged to Success, who had hit his forehead against however many branches, one of which left a neat reverse Nike swoosh cut above his left eye. It's his distinguishing mark into adulthood. The other was the blood Twoboy lost courtesy of a piece of wire used to hold together two rungs on the ladder, which decorated his right cheek with the shape of a bracket. People now use that to distinguish him from his twin brother, Bigboy.

Arthur got up bravely, but immediately found he couldn't walk. His knees gave, and he lay back on the ground, deep pain coursing from his lower back and up his spine. Other than that, he did not spot a bruise though he had quite a significant collection of circumstantial scratches to confirm he had been in some scrape.

Arthur's sisters and Sisi Maka swerved round the corner, skirts flying, in response to the loud commotion. Two of the nearest neighbours' workers also came, out of curiosity, and by the time Arthur's father came, called on the telephone by Arthur's sister, a reasonable crowd of spectators from the township had gathered.

Jairos (typically) says the only other thing that happened was everyone started to cough badly as well. He doesn't know why, but "Arthur's dad gave us all *chotsextractocflectix* and we were fine after just a day". This was a popularly advertised cough mixture whose brand name many people in the township found tongue twisting, perhaps because of the way the voice-over intoned it on radio: "Choats… Extract of Lettuce." Quite how anyone could catch a cold from falling off a tree, only Jairos knows, as this piece of information was not verified by his comrades. They only ignored him, as usual.

The incident wasn't funny at all at the time, but the remnants of *Chikwata* can laugh about it now. Jairos is, in fact, rolling on the floor and his sides are hurting, for he cannot stop laughing and has the last say. "It was embarrassing, when you think about it! Arthur wanted so much to be white and to teach us to play white boy games, make us do white boy stuff." He bends over, clutches his midriff and declares, "It was like walking around the house naked, thinking no one is looking, only to find that the curtains are open!"

Vinnie, Maglobo, Twoboy and Success all glare at him, frowns on their heads. Must be something he heard somewhere and has been desperately trying to find where to fit it. They shake their heads. Vinnie rolls his eyes. Jairos has stopped laughing now but a huge colourless grin remains on his face, like a frozen black-and-white photograph that has seen better days.

Arthur got a hiding from his father and then went into hiding for a whole month. His dad, who is just a regular nice guy, brought in expert carpenters and they used long lasting, treated timber to build a beautiful tree house that tucks neatly into the avocado tree, embedded up there as if it came with the tree. The deck is not a long way up, and you reach it by a short wooden ladder on the north side of the tree. There is only one house with a tree house in its backyard in the whole of Old Highfield. Arthur has bragging rights to it, but he found new friends at the private school he is now attending. His dad made sure of that, having concluded that the *Chikwata from 6Pounds* were no good for his son.

Acknowledgements

I owe a lot of my creative writing today to the many interactions and intimate conversations I had in the formative years of my journalism career with celebrated icons of the writing craft. As an arts reporter and critic, I had the opportunity to get really close and personal with the subjects of my interviews and ended up counting them among my growing network of arts friends and associates. It's been many years since award-winning and internationally-acclaimed author Chenjerai Hove died but it was from him that I learned about the many levels of human interaction and to never take things at face value. I was privileged to read many of his manuscripts before they became published sellout novels, realising only later that he was showing me the writing process as he was always encouraging me to jump onto his literary train. His family became my family and I remain forever indebted to him and grateful for his embrace as his young brother. It was always uplifting sitting around with him and my late Uncle Joe, as they shared rib-tickling stories of animals which talked and sought to outsmart each other.

When Chenjerai Hove told me writing was a lonely undertaking I agreed with him only to sound mature and in tune. I worked in a newsroom full of journalists typing away and our creativity only went as far as finding the best ways to recount a news story. We were not fiction writers, after all. His assertion makes sense now, and I would like to pay tribute to my near-perfect wife, Caroline, who has known to be invisible when I am "in the zone"!

Family has been my greatest pillar of support. I want to thank all the members of the Mawerera family for the cheerleading and, in particular, our children Tina, Chichi and Thobile who have all exhibited huge appetites for books and writing.

My grateful thanks, too, to the current crop of Zimbabwe writers who have come out in support and said, "about time"! and then gone on to demand the next book. Much thanks to accomplished writers Dr Ignatius Mabasa and Memory Chirere, who blew the wind beneath my wings; as well as my longstanding friends, the poet Chirikure Chirikure, crusader of the ever-growing LitFest, the Zimbabwe Literature Festival and distinguished thespian Daves Guzha, founder of Rooftop Promotions and Theatre in the Park.

My final thanks go to my publishers, Carnelian Heart, harsh but constructive critics whose sharp editing eyes made me see things in my writing I had not seen before! Between them and several back-and-forth edits, Samantha Vazhure and Panashe Nyagwambo smoothed out the edges of this project and earned my respect for the professional way they went about it.

About the author

PHOTO CREDIT: DIGSOL MEDIA, ZIMBABWE

The veteran journalist and public relations expert, Ray Mawerera, is a renowned Harare-based media and communications consultant who possesses a deep passion for the arts. This is his second work of fiction. His debut work – a novella exploring the theme of post-traumatic stress titled Zagamo: The War Within – was launched in early 2024 to much critical acclaim. As a journalist of many years' experience, Mawerera became famous in early 1980s-1990s Zimbabwe as a respected arts critic of works of most forms of art, including book, theatre and music reviews. He switched to public relations in the early 1990s when he was offered a senior post in a multinational conglomerate. Over the years, he continued working at executive management level for various large organisations in marketing communications and media and public relations portfolios. He is the current (2025) chairman of arguably Zimbabwe's leading theatre and cultural arts company, Rooftop Promotions, best known for its iconic Theatre in the Park in Harare and short television dramas. He has sat on the Boards of Directors of several public and private institutions. Ray Mawerera lives and works in Harare, where he stays with his wife Caroline. The couple has three children and two grandchildren.

www.ingramcontent.com/pod-product-compliance
Lightning Source LLC
Chambersburg PA
CBHW010436170726
48283CB00011B/3240